STRANGE LABOUR

Editor: Aidan Morgan
Cover art: Paul Klassen
Book and cover design: Tania Wolk, Third Wolf Studio
Printed and bound in Canada at Friesens, Altona, MB
Second Printing 2020
The publisher gratefully acknowledges the support of
Creative Saskatchewan, the Canada Council for the Arts and SK Arts.

Library and Archives Canada Cataloguing in Publication

Title: Strange labour / Robert G. Penner.
Names: Penner, Robert G., author.
Identifiers: Canadiana (print) 20200301616 | Canadiana (ebook) 20200301624 | ISBN 9781989274354
(softcover) | ISBN 9781989274361 (PDF)
Classification: LCC PS8631.E5553 S76 2020 | DDC C813/.6—dc23

radiant press
Box 33128 Cathedral PO
Regina, SK S4T 7X2
info@radiantpress.ca
www.radiantpress.ca

Praise for Strange Labour

"A post-apocalyptic road novel with the gnomic quality of a parable, *Strange Labour* shimmers with a meaning just beyond reach."
– **Sofia Samatar** – author of *A Stranger in Olondria* and *The Winged Histories,* winner of the World Fantasy Award.

"What strange labour are care work and companionship, folkloreing and child-rearing. How obliquely they appear in whatever it is we sometimes call SF. What is it that stops anyone from doing only this social work, only what needs to be done? Robert Penner's wonderful novel brings this work front and centre. A woman wanders the desolate US, stays at a care home, meets a man and travels with him, they briefly stay at a commune of liberal aesthetes, then make their way to a camp named Big Echo. Miranda and Dave, Dave and Miranda, Dave delivering improvisational yarns, Miranda accruing eerie topographic patternings, Dave telling stories, Miranda telling stories. Digging, getting down, they try to avoid the overtly and not so overtly fascistic remnants of what was. Where does that get them? Miranda says to Dave, at one point, that "there is nothing post-apocalyptic about violent men getting what they want". The problems, they are the same. There is nothing post-apocalyptic about this novel. And yet it devastates me."
– **Robert Kiely** – Poet-in-Residence at University of Surrey, Guilford, England.

"Penner proposes an original, quiet apocalypse of labour that resists comprehension; a great metaphor for our socioeconomic predicament. But also much more than that: a bleak, beautiful, even inspiring vision of humanity's future. In what feels like an echo of our post-post-world, human industry–and the mythology around it–is driven to absurdity. This is the evolution of humans into creatures defined by their labour: a new evolutionary directive, a novel organization of the human psyche. The origin story of a new species told from the perspective of those bound for extinction.

Brilliantly, it's the diggers, the non-violent turned, the meek plagued, who are organized and efficient. At least they're building something new. The rest, the survivors, are decaying, self-destructing, clinging uselessly to their ghosts. The novel bears quiet witness to the extinction of the bourgeoisie and the strange labour of an apocalyptic proletariat."
– **Natalia Theodoridou** – winner of the 2018 World Fantasy Award for Short Fiction, 2018 Nebula Award Finalist.

More praise for Strange Labour

"With crystal clear prose and exquisite restraint, *Strange Labour* conjures an apocalypse and an aftermath, the meanings of which are always just beyond reach. As Miranda roadtrips across the US, she meets multiple survivors, all desperate to retain purpose in a world which is no longer and can never again be the same. Can they escape the spectral structures of the past? Do their actions matter? Do ours?"
– **Mark Bould** – author of *The Anthropocene Unconscious*

"What do you do, when it's after the end of the world? What does it mean to survive the annihilation of everything you formerly took for granted? *Strange Labour* offers us a beautiful, wavering meditation on these questions. The novel moves through all the usual post-apocalyptic fantasies -- a romantic road trip among the ruins, a desperate clinging to vestiges of the past, new forms of community -- but it finds all of them wanting. It's a book whose tone continually changes: lucid and observant at some moments, harshly pragmatic at others, and dreamy and dissociated at still others. We are left at the end neither with hope nor despair, but perhaps with a vague sense of making do that is more valuable than either."
– **Steven Shaviro** – SF Critic and author of *The Universe of Things: On Speculative Realism and Discognition.*

"Though Westerners often flock to post-apocalyptic tales for escapist entertainment, this novel takes us where the best literature always does: into the heart of our own darkness. *Strange Labour* is a story about stories—what we tell ourselves, what we tell others, and what kind of endings humans are willing to endure.

Robert Penner has crafted a compelling, disturbing vision, not only of a bleak American future stripped of any real sense of purpose, but of the questionable values and comforting lies defining the current cultural landscape."
– **Chauna Craig** – author of *The Widow's Guide to Edible Mushrooms*, winner of the Next Generation Indie Book Award for Short Fiction.

STRANGE LABOUR

ROBERT G. PENNER

radiant press

Like all commodities this book is the product not
of individual effort but of social relations.
Nonetheless, I owe a special thanks to Nicole,
who said I should write a novel, suggested the topic,
and whose endless enthusiasm and encouragement made
the labour not just possible but pleasurable.
I wrote this story for you.

I

THE TOWN

1

IN HARRISBURG, MIRANDA DECIDED to leave the roads and follow the railway over the Appalachians. She sat on a bench in the empty station for over an hour, admiring the blunt-nosed profile of an abandoned locomotive, before she hopped from the platform down onto the tracks and walked out of that deserted place. Soon she came upon the Susquehanna, a shining highway, silver in the early evening light, sweeping beneath a stone bridge that seemed a mile across. On the far bank the gloomy hills rose up from the ruined pastoral, a collection of giant heads, crooked elbows, and bent knees.

She had been looking forward to the views as she climbed up into the cadaverous landscape but was disappointed. Over the next few days there were only occasional glimpses through the trees of the land sinking away into uncertain depths. Once, where a rickety viaduct carried the tracks across a road, she saw, framed by the forest, a rolling horizon almost black against the washed out sky. Later, looking back down a hairpin turn, she was enthralled by a shifting world of fog and cloud, pierced here and there by shafts of light, but in general her hours were spent staring at close grey skies and closer walls of bark, branch, and dripping leaves.

Sometimes she walked right down the middle of the tracks,

trusting long-dead engineers to pick out the most efficient path through the wilderness. Sometimes, when the stuttering steps she took from tie to tie were tripping her up, she trudged through the slushy drifts that lay between the embankments and the trees. In the wet winter, her pants were perpetually soaked from ankle to thigh, but she had found a pair of good hiking boots in the backroom tumble of a looted shoe store somewhere in New Jersey, and they kept her feet perfectly dry on the long trudge up and over the broken back of the mountains.

One afternoon she found an old industrial building, a crumbling complex of brick, steel, and concrete squatting in a clearing across a run and a ragged road. Attached to that haphazard constellation was a water tower and, as soon as she had clambered through the muddy ditches and scaled the fence, she began to climb it. Above the trees the wind hissed wildly in her ears and clawed at her knuckles. Her boots kept slipping on the icy rungs. At about fifty feet off the ground she stuck her arm through the ladder, hooked her elbow around the side rail, and twisted about. The pale sun hung ghostly over the wooded hills. She searched the sky for contrails, listened for engines, scanned the vacant expanse for smoke, clouds of dust, steam, exhaust, but there was nothing, just a colorless sprawl of trees and rock.

The building was filled with rusting cauldrons, each big enough to boil a hippopotamus whole, titanic chains forged from iron cables as thick as her wrists, long metallic reefs of steps, scaffolding, walkways, imponderable machines stuck fast, rubber belts and rotting gears crusted over with calcium and dust. She spent the night there, sleeping on an office floor, burning chipboard for warmth.

She ran out of food as she began the descent and shot a squirrel with the .22. A corrugated steel culvert provided enough shelter for her to roast it over a small fire. There were no birds. The ground was a mess of dirty snow and decomposing leaves. When the clouds passed over the sun black-and-white bands rushed across the forest floor. Miranda burned her fingers tugging the meat from the delicate bones. Once picked clean she buried the carcass under the ash of the fire.

It was like a medieval painting of a village in winter: trees marching right into the settlement, tidy houses perched on the hill sides, a steeple, the hint of streets under the snow: a pocket of fragile order coalesced out of chaos, holding steady against encroachment. The people were missing of course – the reassuring busyness of the peasants and the burghers was not there to give the scene energy – but the dogs were there, a half dozen or so sniffing around in front of a pharmacy: lean, dark hounds, once loved and overconfident, now wary and suspicious.

Miranda watched them for a while from where the railway emerged out of its wilderness. She slung the .22 from her shoulder, loosened the .45 in her belt, and allowed herself to slip down the gravel embankment into the ankle-deep snow. The dogs turned to look, ears perked, noses pointing, concentrating themselves, poised. As she approached, they slunk low to the ground, shoulders hunched, hackles raised. She could hear them growling.

"Go!" she shouted. "Go home!"

They began to bark and she shot into the air. A burst of pigeons exploded from a rooftop and the dogs fled. The crack echoed up and down the street, up the hills and into the woods.

Miranda walked up to the pharmacy and checked the door. It was open and she let herself in. Someone had already been there. Most of the shelves were swept clean. Bottles and boxes littered the floor. She closed the door behind her and locked it. The space in the back where they kept all the good stuff was thoroughly rummaged, but she found some Claritin and Sudafed that had fallen behind a counter. That kind of thing was sometimes good for trade.

She stuck her head out the back. The parking lot was full of snow, and a light blue Honda Civic, the sides spotted with rust and the top hidden under a blanket of white, was the only vehicle nearby. She wiped a window clean and peered in. She walked around the back and with the tip of her boot brushed the license plate clean. Pennsylvania. There were dog and deer tracks in the lane. There was a second door in the back wall of the pharmacy with a mailbox beside it. Miranda tried it, but it was locked. She went back into the pharmacy and searched for a key. After about a half hour she found one in a desk drawer. She also found the keys for the Civic. When she stepped back outside a reddish terrier with matted hair was watching her.

She tried the car first but couldn't get a wheeze out of the motor. The apartment door was swollen and stiff, but she shouldered it open, then locked it behind her. At the top of the steps was a well-kept but musty apartment. Dust covered everything. The shelves were full of photo albums and secondhand books: self-help, potboilers, and thrillers. Miranda searched the place, then opened a can of beans from the pantry and ate it over the sink. She went to the bedroom and threw her pack on the floor, leaned the .22 against the wall, pushed a dresser in front of the door, and took off her boots. The window overlooked the street. The dogs were already back, noses in her tracks, tails wagging, intent on the smell of her. She drew the curtains shut, pushed the dresser out of the way, and padded out. She returned with a book and pushed the dresser back, lay down on the bed and started reading. She was asleep in minutes, the book beside her, the spine cracked from age and use.

She woke once in the middle of the night to the sound of a dog fight.

The next day she poked around in the nearby shops and apartments. The dogs followed her at a distance, and she suspected it was from hunger rather than malice. She found bottled water, socks, thermal underwear, and a fully loaded bar. She went back to the apartment above the pharmacy where she scrounged up enough furniture to start a blazing fire in the parking lot. She filled all the bowls, pots, and buckets she could find with snow and put them near the flames. While she waited for the melt water to boil she heated up an open can of beans and franks in the coals. She sat in the Civic, poked around in the glovebox, checked herself out in the mirror and saw the terrier sitting in the back lane watching her. When the beans were steaming she dug out a few spongy chunks of meat and tossed them to the animal before she ate the rest.

It was hard work running up and down the stairs to fill the tub.

She finally found a body. There was always a body, sometimes two or three. This one was in a church. People often seemed to go to churches to die. It was a woman in a bright blue dress with a gold brooch on the chest, a veiled hat crooked on her iron-grey hair, a prayer book and a clutch on the bench beside her, withered skin blasted to her skull, shovel teeth pushing through her lips. She must have closed the door against the dogs. Miranda sat with her awhile.

There was a small library by the courthouse. Light streamed in through high windows, lighting up the universe of dust motes suspended in the thick air. Most of the books were heavy hardcovers but Miranda eventually found a small carousel of paperbacks that included a half dozen or so of the old-fashioned Penguins with the orange spine. She selected a few – The Midwich Cuckoos, Monkey Planet, The Singing Grass – and stuffed them into her backpack. Then she browsed the magazine section for a while until she had a sizeable stack of Vogue, Elle, and People. She lugged them to a table in the sun and flipped through them. The images were a mad garden of shapes and colors and she ran her fingers over the glossy pages, smiling at how many of the names she could recall without reading the captions. As the sun sank, the shadows crept across the table and the floor, crawling up the wall, and the library became cool and gloomy. Miranda chose a particularly fat Vogue with a blonde woman in a red dress on the cover posing with the Statue of Liberty, and she slipped it into the backpack with the books.

It was cold out. Wet snow was falling and dark clouds were drifting in over the hills. Miranda stopped at the bar on the way home and got drunk on beer and whiskey, broke into the vending and cigarette machines, and had a little party until the room was too dark to be enjoyable. It was late evening when she finally staggered out. She steadied herself against the wall. The clouds were gone and a giant moon hung over the little town. The dogs were on the other side of the street, eyes glittering in the shadows.

"Go away," she shouted. "Go home!"

They didn't move until she did. Then they trailed after her, keeping their distance, but slinking closer whenever she wasn't watching. She kept catching herself speeding up.

"Don't run," she muttered. "Don't run."

She stumbled and felt them tense with anticipation. She lurched ahead, stopped short, and spun around to catch a black Lab creeping in close, belly brushing the ground, no more than five feet behind her.

"Go!" she shouted. "Go home!"

It barked loudly and a couple of others joined in. Miranda pulled out the .45 and waved it about.

"Go home," she said. "Go home!"

She fired it into the ground.

White eyes rolled, fangs naked in pink gums, deep throaty growls. A yellow mutt darted past her and she spun, slipped, and threw herself against the wall. There was a half-circle of them hemming her in. It happened so fast she barely saw them move; Labs, Retrievers, an Alsatian, a couple of mutts. A surge of adrenaline washed her senses clean: the stars glittered in the black puddles. Countless horrifying eyes. Rank acid fear soaked her armpits and back. She smelled the raw meat hunger of the dogs. She slid along the wall, pointing the gun at the Alsatian.

The pack followed her, a single shifting scuttling terror. Behind her she felt a glass shop door and she pushed on it with the flat of her foot. It swung open and bells tinkled overhead. She backed into darkness, closing the door as she did. The words Erie Insurance Company were stenciled on the outside glass. One of the dogs started barking. The others joined together in a rough deafening chorus. She found the lock, turned it, and pulled down the blinds. She stumbled about in the dark until she found a leather couch and collapsed on it. The raucous noise outside eventually faded and she lay the gun down on the floor beside her.

She woke up shaking with cold, in pitch darkness, to a hound's mournful howling. Not far away, maybe a block or two. She imagined herself driving the Honda Civic down the main street, sliding about on the ice and snow, running down the dogs as they fled, one by one.

2

THE HIGHWAY THAT COILED its way down the Allegheny Escarpment was littered with deserted vehicles, many with doors open just as the drivers and passengers left them, keys still in the ignition. The gas had evaporated or gone stale ages ago, but they were still useful places to spend the night, out of the wind and safe from feral dogs and wild animals. Miranda would scrounge up wood and start a fire a foot or two from the door to warm herself before bed, maybe boil some water for tea, or make broth from a bouillon cube. One night she woke up in a Cadillac Seville and heard something snuffling about outside her car. The door at her feet was still open and she cautiously reached out and as quietly as she could she swung it shut. The snuffling stopped and she lay there shivering in the cold, listening, until the thin pre-sunrise light relieved her anxiety and she fell back asleep. When she woke a second time, she had a look around and found a bear's pawprint pressed into the muddy shoulder a few yards away.

There were deer, of course, especially in the morning and the evenings, drifting in little groups, in and out of the trees, past the cars and the trucks, turning small heads on long necks to stare at Miranda, indifferent to her, calm. She would have made good time, whatever that meant now, but it rained a lot. It was as if, as the hills receded into the distance, the clouds rushed in to fill the vacuum. She spent quite a few hours huddled up in cars, listening to the rattle of the rain on the roof and the road, reading her new books, fitfully napping, daydreaming.

There were many little towns and villages along the highway. Clusters of houses clung to the slopes like lichen on rocks, sprouted in the valleys. There was never a problem finding food or holing up in a bed for the night. Now that she was out of the rough country with its scarps of stone and trees she often had a horizon, and sometimes spotted clouds of dust or smoke in the distance. Once, she heard the distant buzz of a combustion engine, but it faded into silence before she could pinpoint its direction. Once, she found motorcycle tracks on one of the dirt roads that fed the highway. They were no more than a few days old. She decided not to investigate the neighborhood and continued her descent towards the Midwest and the Great Lakes. Once, she heard the crack of a firearm, and she listened, wide-eyed and nauseous with surprise, to the reverberations.

The railway she had previously walked along crossed and re-crossed her new road, and these intersections were crowded with maintenance sheds, brick warehouses with broken windows, and crooked clapboard homes toppling in on themselves. Every vertical surface was decorated with hieroglyphic graffiti, meaningless icons, cave paintings inspired by extinct emotions. Miranda walked past row after row of deserted railcars coupled together in rusting chains, past box stores and credit unions and fast food restaurants, parking lots still filled with commuter vehicles, Methodist chapels and Catholic churches,

Freemason Halls, coffee shops and bars and pharmacies empty of life. On one occasion she saw the onion bulbs of an Orthodox cathedral rising like Byzantium from a sea of derelict roofs. It was all detritus now, empty accumulations, rubble. It made her think of the ruins of Rome in the Dark Ages. She recalled fragments of translated Anglo-Saxon verse: descriptions of solitary wanderers in deserted landscapes, wealth laid waste, grey windswept walls stained with red, crumbling at the touch of frost. She thought of peasants grazing their sheep in the Colosseum, gentlemen on their Grand Tour enthralled by Piranesi, jetlagged tourists taking photographs in the crypts.

At one of those intersections she found a sturdily built hiking trail, not yet completely overgrown, and for half a day she followed it down into a valley where it meandered along, sometimes after the highway, sometimes after the train tracks. Occasionally it would sweep out into the bush and take her past even older structures than those she was used to; icy cairns of piled bricks that had once been blast furnaces, coal carts abandoned like bodies in the bush, isolated railway bridges cutting across gullies crowded with yellow marrowed trees, a grist wheel twisted into a lemniscate. When she reached a place where she could choose between clambering back up to the desolate highway through a few feet of scrubby new growth, or plunging down with the path into a dark, dripping crevasse that stank of mushrooms, vegetal decay and sulfur, she chose the more recent catastrophe.

Miranda climbed a fence into a schoolyard and explored the empty classrooms, desks still in neat rows, lessons half-finished on the whiteboards, a cup ringed with coffee sedimentation on the principal's desk. The gymnasium walls were crenellated with high windows and shafts of dusty light illuminated basketballs, scattered about like eggs dug out of a giant lizard's nest. She threw her bags down at the door and shot hoops for a half hour, dribbling about the key, twisting, turning, the sound of the ball hitting the floor a sharp, stinging slap. She launched fade away after fade away, shot after shot drifting through the air in long, lazy arcs.

Near a cloverleaf interchange someone had hung the bodies of a half-dozen dogs from a tree. Most of them were dried husks, but one of them was still raw, with wet eyes and a protruding tongue. Behind the tree was a pile of their predecessor's skulls. Three wolf traps were staked in the underbrush nearby, baited with hunks of rotting meat. The shoulder and verge were crisscrossed with motorcycle tracks. Miranda looked around but saw no smoke, no houses nearby, no signs of life but a murmuration of starlings winding and unwinding itself in the misty air. She found a long, twisted branch about as thick as her thumb and set off the traps. They snapped shut with a loud crack, each one taking a foot off the end of her prod. She hurried away, heart pounding, sweating despite the cold, frequently glancing over her shoulder until the interchange was well out of sight.

The next day she heard an engine approaching from behind and darted off the road into the trees. Someone on a dirt bike came bombing up the highway, helmeted head turning to and fro, slowing down by the vehicles to peer in, or gazing into the bush on either side, black visor blank. They had a shotgun on their back. Above the headlight they had mounted a dog skull, from which the handle bars seemed to sprout like horns. Miranda hid until the bike passed by and the sound of it died away. She walked a mile or two more down the highway until it occurred to her that the dog killer could have wheeled their vehicle off the road and hidden themselves in the brush as she had. She deserted the highway again and scratched out a little camp over a rise and rested there in the cold until she heard a bike come buzzing back the other way. She made a little fire and had some tea, ate some stale crackers, then went on her way.

Over the next few days her anxiety about the dog killer faded into a sort of ache. The towns were more frequent than they had been, and more abandoned buildings were piled right up next to the roads that ran between them: gas stations, diners, car dealerships, factories and chemical plants with their annexes and chemical tanks and rudimentary outbuildings, girlie bars, adult video stores, shooting ranges, and industrial goods outlets. The wildlife changed as well. More dogs again, wary shadows trailing after her, the constant stink of cat piss at every camp, raccoons humping across the road on their midnight raids, rats scuttling along the joints of wall and parking lot, crows and ravens haunting the dumpsters, and once, a huge mottled pig watched her pass from the side of the road, bat ears twitching. It simply squatted there, a massive lump of hair, meat, and cartilage that had persisted and prospered through all the changes. Miranda thought briefly of murdering it for its indifference and butchering it on the spot, but she hated this stretch of the road so much she did not want to stop.

Eventually the lingering evidence of all that post-industrial despair was disrupted by an airport, a rectangle of runways parallel to the highway, rigid geometries giving way to a creeping blur of weeds and bush on the far side, and beyond that a forest. It was a relief to see such deliberate artifice in the wilderness, so she crunched through the thinly iced ditch, cut across the shoulder and berm, skirted the chain link fence, and walked right out onto the cracked concrete. She wandered through the parked aircraft. The Cessnas and Pipers were empty-eyed and fragile looking. There was a helicopter too, rotors loose and slumping. She climbed inside and sat in the pilot's seat, experimenting with the levers and pedals. When she glanced in the back she saw that one of the side doors had been left open. Mice had gotten inside and torn up the seats to make their nests. The floor was littered with their turds.

After the airport the land became a mix of woods and farmland, teetering old barns and Quonset sheds, fences and gates. Here she finally came across one of the diggings. The road curved around a low bluff past which the whole world opened up: low hills entirely denuded, carved into a sprawling, curling network of earthen mounds and grooves, muddy trenches deep and wide enough to accommodate a semitrailer. It was the same incomprehensible, labyrinthine network Miranda had seen so many times on the eastern seaboard. Nonetheless, she was surprised; until now the Appalachians had seemed free of the diggings, and she had not heard the telltale rumblings of the heavy equipment the diggers used. The absence here of the men and women responsible for the earthworks intrigued Miranda. She walked across the muddy border that lay between the highway and the diggings and trudged up to the crest of the closest mound.

She followed its weaving path to the top of the hill, peering down into ditches that ran along either side of her, the sticky clay at their bottoms churned up into tracks by the big machines that had carved them out. On the other side of the hill the trenches and mounds tapered off. The valley beyond was stripped clean, a once-hidden brook exposed to the elements, but the real work of digging and mound building had not yet begun here – the earth was bare and smooth. Miranda hiked down into the valley, her heavy breath visible. She waded through the weedy run and climbed the next rise as well. Thick mud clung to her boots but she was sure there must be a camp somewhere nearby, so she struggled to the top. She was right. The clearcutting resolved into bush in the next valley. The yellow bulldozers were motionless among the trees at the edge of the bare clay and a partially loaded logging truck was parked next to a massive tangle of uprooted trees. Once Miranda was near enough, she could see weeds poking through the tractor treads. There were some tents in the woods, and lean-tos jury-rigged from blue tarps and rebar. Bodies were scattered about in the underbrush, torn apart and picked over, dragged halfway out of the tents, mostly skeletal, but some were withered mummies in their clothes. She examined a few of them closely, looking for gunshot wounds or blunt force trauma, but it all looked like post-mortem damage to her.

Dust to dust.

She was almost certain it was not violence that visited these people, but famine or disease or maybe just exhaustion. She had seen that often enough. Near the heavy equipment, the bodies were few and scattered, but as she made her way deeper into the trees they occurred in clusters. She even found the remains of a few small children tangled up with the adults. It looked like it was once a well-organized encampment. Tents were arranged in groups, there were porta-potty stations, and in the clearings, rings of picnic tables around the charred mounds of cooking fires. No smell of decomposition tainted the frozen air, and some tendrils and shoots had begun to creep over the corpses before winter arrested their growth. A few birds fluttered about nervously in the trees, and a few paw prints could be found here and there. They looked like dog to Miranda. What a feast for the few scavengers who had found this place. Miranda reached the outer limits of the encampment after a short, slow walk. The trees grew closer together at the edge, the underbrush thicker, the shadows deeper. Wind moved through the canopy: it whispered, the trees moaned. Miranda shivered at the cliché.

3

A BLIZZARD HIT AS MIRANDA arrived in a small town. More than a blizzard: it felt to her as if the full frozen horror of the void shattered the sky and blasted through the streets. Miranda leaned into the acid burn of the arctic wind for a block or two, battered, stung by the snow, barely able to get enough oxygen out of the air. She broke into a restaurant with two stories of apartments above it. She searched the commercial pantry then made her way to the top floor.

Operatic winds howled for two days. Demons circled, beams creaked, walls quivered, draughts cycled about the floors, windows became sheets of creeping ice. Miranda shivered under layers of blankets, eating canned ravioli and peaches, breaking the clear, brittle crusts of ice with a spoon, keeping cans of beer from freezing with her body warmth.

On the third day she woke up to white light streaming in through the fractal whorls of the frosted windows. She forced one of the windows open and was staggered by the sunlight: the sky was a brilliant blue, the buildings that lined the street were rich red brick, and banks of sparkling snow covered the streets. She bundled up and went downstairs but the snow was piled so high she couldn't get the front door or the fire escape to budge.

As she stood there considering her situation she heard a faint cry from outside, thin and querulous. She ran up the stairs to the second floor landing and yanked open a window.

An old man across the street was picking his way through the troughs between the snow banks. He wore a blue hospital robe and pajama bottoms. His grey hair was cropped short, a few days growth on his chin.

"Marigold!" he shouted. "Marigold!"

He fell over, staggered to his feet, and stumbled on, leaving a slipper behind, plunging his socked foot into the snow.

"Marigold!"

Miranda looked around. The street was otherwise empty. He had broken a meandering channel through the snow, down the middle of the road from the outskirts of town in the direction she had come from. She ran upstairs and grabbed some blankets, paused, picked up the .22, then ran back down to the second floor window and peered out.

The old man was gone. She fought the window all the way up, tossed the blankets and the rifle out, then slung herself over the edge, hung there for a second, feeling the wind on her knuckles, the frozen stone against her hands, the hard brick at her knees. She let herself drop.

She found him in a gift store, huddled up in the farthest corner and shaking.

"Marigold?" he said when he saw her. "Is that you, Marigold?"

She lay the slipper she had collected down and wrapped a blanket around him. He started to cough. It was a raw, phlegmy rasp. She peeled off his wet sock and dried his foot with the corner of a blanket. She took off her boot, removed one of her own socks and rolled it up over his cool, waxy flesh.

The old man was shaking violently, eyes tightly closed.

"What's your name?" Miranda asked as she laced her boot back up. He said nothing, just sat and shook.

"Where do you live?"

He opened his eyes and glared at her. They were very blue.

"What?" he snapped. "Who are you? Where's Marigold?"

Miranda sat back on her haunches. He glared at her and then subsided back into his shivering. She began poking around for something to start a fire in. She found the stairs to the basement and had ducked down into the musty shadows, in the hope of finding a metal mop bucket, when she heard the front door open and someone call out.

"Arthur," a woman shouted. "Arthur! Where are you?"

Miranda froze. Her .22 was still up there, laid flat across a shelf.

"Arthur! What are you doing?"

The voice fell silent and the floorboards creaked. Miranda crept to the foot of the stairs. After a few minutes, the woman called out again:

"Hullo! Hullo!"

"Is anyone here?"

"Hullo?"

The floorboards creaked again. The woman was at the top of the stairs, a silhouette, heavy-set, glasses glimmering.

"Hullo?"

"Hullo?"

"If you are down there I just wanted to let you know we're at the nursing home up near the Catholic Church, north east of here. You'll see the smoke if you walk back up Main Street. We have good food. Not from cans. We got ham from real pigs. And beans. And cabbage. You're welcome to come up and eat as much as you'd like. You can even fill your rucksack."

The floorboards groaned.

"Come on, Arthur. Let's get you home."

"Marigold?" Arthur called out, voice cracking.

"No, honey, Marigold's not here."

Miranda's blankets were rolled up neatly in the corner. The rifle propped where she left it. She walked over to the front door and peered out. The woman was dragging Arthur on a bright red plastic sled straight up the middle of Main Street, up past Miranda's building, heading northeast. Miranda watched until they were out of sight and then followed them. Their tracks kept going out of town towards the highway and then swung left and vanished in the trees at the foot of a hill. At the top of the hill was a modern church, a massive wedge of concrete, steel and glass, flashing in the cold sun. About halfway up the hill, between Miranda and the church, a column of white smoke, thick as treacle, rose out of the woods.

Miranda crept up and watched the place for the rest of the afternoon. It was a four-story apartment block overlooking the playing fields of a nearby school or community center. The only person who came in and out was the woman. There was a roughly made chicken coop in the parking lot and a giant pile of coal under a tarp. Miranda spent a lot of time thinking about those chickens as she watched, about how fat they were. She spent a lot of time thinking about the eggs that were surely there. In the evening a large lounge or common room behind floor-to-ceiling windows was lit up with candles. A half-dozen elderly people sat at the tables and lay in beds that had been used to transform the room into a dormitory. She returned to the apartment where she had weathered the storm and dug her way back in through the snowdrifts.

Miranda lay shivering in the dark, overcome with anxiety so intense it felt close to panic. She tried to formulate greetings in her head, introductory sentences, witticisms with which to break the ice. She could not remember the last time she spoke to someone else. New Jersey? Philadelphia? It had been some time before Harrisburg. She had met a young couple trailing after the diggers. They had not been able to explain why. Their thick southern accents hadn't helped matters. The man in particular was difficult to understand. He would stare at her intensely as he talked, like he was willing her to make sense of the sounds coming out of his mouth, but she felt like she could only recognize every third or fourth word. At the time she felt like she was going mad, losing her senses. She felt stupid. The couple had been kind and cheerful enough. There was plenty of laughter shared between them. But the sight of them bending their heads together over their meals, washing their camp plates and dishes, the quiet words exchanged, the sight of all that tenderness caused Miranda an intense embarrassment. Almost shame. She felt the same feeling of shame when she watched the woman light the candles in that room full of old folks, as they all puttered about in their quiet intimacy.

Still, thought Miranda, those chickens, those eggs.

The next morning, just as the sun was creeping up over the hills, she approached the woman as she was about to start feeding her hens.

"Hullo," said Miranda and the woman looked up.

She had a wool cap pulled down over a large head, grey hair curling around the edges; big, round glasses; small nose; round cheeks rosy with broken capillaries; shorter than Miranda but broader.

"You must be the guardian angel from the gift shop," the woman said. The chickens began to mutter impatiently.

"I guess I must be," said Miranda.

The woman pushed her glasses up her nose and squinted at Miranda.

"Let me finish up here," she turned back to her anxious birds. "Then we can have breakfast."

It was glorious.

Three eggs basted in bacon fat, glossy whites crisp around the edges. Fat yolks barely constrained, yielding briefly to the point of a knife before the puncture. Creamy gold spilling over fried potatoes. A thick salty slab of slightly glutinous ham. A mug of sweet, steaming tea. Neither of them spoke as they ate.

When Miranda was finally finished, she leaned back in her chair.

"So," said the woman. "I am Esther. Who are you?"

"Miranda."

They sat in silence.

"Would you like some more tea?"

"No, thank you."

Miranda luxuriated in the lingering smells. Esther watched her. Finally, Miranda pushed her chair back and stood up.

"Thank you," she said. "I'll be going now."

Esther followed her to the door and down the hall to the foyer. When Miranda stepped through the glass doors into the cold air, Esther cleared her throat.

"If you are willing to work, you can stay as long as you like," she said. "There are plenty of empty apartments. And plenty of food."

"What kind of work?" Miranda asked.

"There are five old folk still here – all senile. The others left with the rest of them, went out to the diggings on the Cone-maugh. They all left if they could, the old ones, or died here, except my five, they never seemed to have the urge to dig. Nor did I."

Miranda waited through the pause.

"I need help with the cooking and the cleaning," said Esther. "And Arthur is always wandering off. Plus there's the scaven-ging."

Miranda and Esther hardly talked, but they made it a habit to take their meals together: eggs, potatoes, ham, cabbage, and plenty of canned tomato soup. The old folks were kept in what was previously the visitor's lounge: Arthur, Mary, Betty, Jimmy,

Joyce. Esther had set up cots along the inside wall and tables and chairs along the windows where they sat. They watched the chickens in the snow, or stared at their hands, or fiddled about with puzzles. Esther and Miranda cleaned them up every morning and evening as best they could with a tub full of well water heated up on a coal burner.

The second afternoon she was there Esther sent Miranda down into town with the red sled to scavenge for bullets and pharmaceuticals.

"For trade," she said. "There's a Mennonite who comes around in the spring with a wagon."

After that, Miranda went every third or fourth afternoon. Sometimes she took Arthur along: bundled up, bony nose protruding from scarves, heavy mitts duct taped on.

"Marigold!" he would holler through his muffler. "Marigold!"

Occasionally he would fall off the sled and Miranda would pile him back on. Sometimes he would make a break for it and Miranda would gently corral him, let him vent for a few minutes, and then get him settled down. Sometimes he would start to weep and Miranda would turn around and pull him home before she set out again. But mostly he was content if they were busy and didn't stay too long in one place.

It was good work, walking those quiet, orderly streets with Arthur in tow. In each house, Miranda would let him wander about the living rooms and kitchens while she raided medicine cabinets, pantries, bedrooms, sheds, and basements. Esther had given her a list of medications to look for: antipsychotics, antidepressants, anti-inflammatories, Enbrel for arthritis, memantin for Alzheimer's, pregabalin, opioids, amphetamines, pseudoephedrine. In the evenings, after the old folks were put to bed, Esther would sort through the take. Most of the Enbrel and the memantin she would assign to the locked pantry in the visitor's lounge, along with assorted anti-inflammatories if they were running low. She would pick over the antipsychotics thoroughly, looking for clozapine, which she would keep for her own use. Miranda would store the rest in the basement with the accumulating ammunition, the linen and toilet paper and paper towels, the hams, the potatoes, the rows and rows and rows of canned goods that made Miranda think of Andy Warhol and latchkey lunches when she was a kid.

Miranda and Arthur were in a big house on the hill, filled with high-end furniture and electronics. The en suite bathroom held a cornucopia of antidepressants. After she filled up her backpack, Miranda went through the walk-in closet. The clothes were beautiful, many clearly bought in a city, or perhaps even abroad. They were all a few sizes too small for Miranda but she looked through them anyway, testing the fabrics between her thumb and forefinger, sometimes rubbing them against her cheeks. A red silk dress was slung over a chair in the corner, when Miranda picked it up and held it to her face, she was convinced she could detect the faintest echo of a rich, floral musk. She closed her eyes and inhaled deeply and the room spun slowly around her, the house, the whole world spun, and she could hear the clink of ice in lowballs and the echo of laid-back jazz and a woman's throaty laugh on the other side of a door.

On the way home she shot a couple of rabbits. Arthur held them on his lap, rubbing the fur this way and that, staring into their blank eyes, singing softly to himself.

A few days later, they were working a more modest street that ran across the hill below the house with the red silk dress. Miranda found Arthur inconsolable in the kitchen of a run-down bungalow she had just finished looting. He was holding a photograph tightly in his crooked fingers. He had plucked it from the fridge. A strong-jawed middle-aged woman in a pantsuit stood in a park or a garden. Her salt-and-pepper hair was cut sensibly short. She smiled for the camera.

"Is that Marigold, Arthur?" Miranda asked, but he just sobbed. "Does she look like Marigold?"

He refused to put it aside for his mitts so she let him hold it in his bare hands all the way back home.

Esther was irritated.

"He could have gotten frostbite," she said when she examined his raw, red hands. "Again."

"I didn't have the heart to take it away. It might have been someone he knew."

Esther rolled her eyes.

"He's got a whole shoe box of middle-aged women under his bed," she said. "Not one of them looks like the other, yet he has wept like a big baby over each and every one."

Miranda shrugged.

"Still," she said. "I didn't want to ruin his moment."

4

ESTHER WAS DISGUSTED THAT MIRANDA named the chickens: Judas, Rosebud, Marzipan, Victoria, Fare-thee-well, Marshmallow, Little Mouse, and Rocket.

"They are not pets," she snapped the first time she heard Miranda call to one.

"No," agreed Miranda. "Not pets."

"Sentimental."

"Yes," cooed Miranda. "So sentimental, aren't we sentimental, Marzipan? Aren't we, Marshmallow? Aren't we sentimental?"

It was Miranda who fed them now. She scattered corn on the snow and they huffed and puffed about her feet, balls of rust and brown and black feathers, red combs like tumors, lizard feet and beady, poisonous eyes. She collected the smooth brown eggs from beneath their roosts, wiping off the occasional smear of shit or blood or wet down, and held them in the palms of her hands before she put them in her bowl, one by one, luxuriating in their fading warmth, in their weight, their sterility. Esther would stare out the window at Miranda flirting with the birds and frown, draw her lips thin.

The chickens were a frequent subject of conversation: their health, their appetites, their behavior. Esther dreamed of getting a rooster.

"If we had a rooster," she frequently said, "we could afford to kill one now and again."

"The nuns need a priest," Miranda would always reply.

"What?" Esther would say.

"Nothing," said Miranda, and then, "Do you think a roast chicken or a stew first?"

And at this point in their catechism her mouth would begin to water.

"Roast chicken," was Esther's response. "Then into the pot with the carcass and a stock for noodle soup."

"Which one?"

"The short fat Rhode Island Red, the one with the bad temper."

"Victoria," Miranda would sigh and glance sidelong at Esther. "Poor Victoria. Poor, fat Victoria."

The older woman would roll her eyes.

Every day, water had to be hauled up from the ancient hand pump at the edge of the property. Every day, the old folks needed to be helped through their meals and the aftermath managed. Esther always did the cooking so Miranda did the dishes. Then there was personal hygiene: water to heat up, faces and hands to be washed, hair brushed and occasionally cut, toiletries attended. The common room and the hallways on the main floor were cleaned every second day with the carpet sweeper, the inside windows washed on the alternates, the toilets and bathrooms every day. And at least once a week, regardless of their condition, they washed the floors in the big institutional kitchen beside the common room. The linen also, once a week:

"On Wednesdays," Esther always insisted and Miranda would smile.

"What?" Esther would snap.

"I've long lost track," Miranda would reply.

"Well, I have not," Esther would say, "lost track."

The common room had a reclining chair, with a reading lamp from which a candle lantern was hung if it was gloomy. You could sit there and look out at the hills receding into the horizon. Esther would put her feet up for a few minutes after lunch and stare out at the black-and-white landscape, maybe read a Bible verse or two, maybe fall asleep. The old folks sat at their beds or the long tables. Mary and Betty might work at an endless puzzle, sliding pieces about, clicking them into place. Joyce would come to chatter at Miranda in the kitchen, to warn her about the dangers in the cellar – "don't go down there alone, don't go down there with Uncle Reg." Arthur would mutter and pace.

When Miranda finished the dishes, she would make a big pot of tea and carry it out. It did not take her long to learn who took what, and once everyone else was set-up, she would bring a cup over to Esther – two sugar and a spoonful of powdered milk.

If Esther was asleep, square head at an angle, delicate rosacea flowering on each cheek, chapped hands clawed on her lap, Miranda would put the cup beside her, throw a quilt over her lap, and find something to do. If Esther was awake, they would sit for a while and chat about the household, about who was out of temper, who seemed ill, what needed to be done, what Esther had planned for the immediate future. They only discussed their pasts once.

"Where were you?" Esther asked on that occasion. She was knitting a yellow sweater. Miranda often teased her about the knitting – "Why scavenge for yarn when you can scavenge for the thing itself? I'd be happy to find you a cozy pair of socks the next time I go out." – but Esther never took the bait. It was soothing for both of them: the flash of the needles in the lamplight, the soft clicking like rain against a window, the sedimentary growth of the rows, and in this instance, the relaxation it induced was so total that Esther broached the subject of the world before.

Miranda looked up from her tea: "Where was I when?"

"When it happened."

"I was working. In the city. In New York. I had started a new job. I was an actuarial accountant with a big firm."

Esther snorted.

Miranda ignored her.

"I looked up and the office was emptying. For a second I thought it was an evacuation but there were no alarms. Then I thought it was lunch but the time was wrong. Some kind of meeting I had forgotten about, maybe. I opened my office door and called out but everyone ignored me. A couple of blank stares like you can get sometimes. You know. Off they all filed. So I walked over to the exit and saw the hallway was filled, packed, everyone heading for the stairs. Salmon up the stream. I stopped someone I knew and asked them what was happening. A colleague. He listened to me patiently and when I was finished with my questions he turned away into the shuffling queue. It was so silent. No one talking."

Miranda took a sip of tea.

"So I walked over to a window and looked out and I could see people filling up the streets. On the Brooklyn Bridge all the cars had stopped and the people were walking into the city to join the exodus. Everyone heading west. To the mainland. It made me think of 9/11, of refugees, of cattle herded toward the slaughterhouse, everyone walking away from a catastrophe, or to a catastrophe. But there was no catastrophe. I checked the radio, I checked CNN, MSNBC, everything. Just dead air and empty desks. Then back to the window and the streets were full, the bridge an absolute throng. I was in shock I think. It made no sense. It took me a while to remember the phone, but no one was picking up. Eventually I joined the silent queue to the stairs and made my way down. I had to walk against the crowd to get home. What struck me was how slow it was, their movement, so many trickles and rivulets and streams forming that implacable river. So many long stops and slow starts. Lots of crying kids following their parents. And I saw a homeless guy I'd seen around before. He was walking against the flow as well but when I called out to get his attention, he ran away. I often wonder how many people like us, how many of the unaffected went along with it, joined the masses because they couldn't think of what else to do, how many people saw me but were too frightened or bewildered to say anything. The sense of loneliness in those early days was overpowering. It was horrifying. It was so silent. The traffic stopped. In New York City. It was so silent. So inhuman. Mostly you just heard the wind, birds, the endless shuffle of feet on concrete. That shuffle sounded to me like a giant snake sloughing its skin."

The knitting needles flashed.

"It must have taken a week for the city to empty. People walking day and night. Even after the power went, they kept walking in the dark. I mostly watched from my apartment but sometimes I'd go down and try to talk to people. Look for others like me who weren't part of it. I kept calling my folks every couple of hours until the phones stopped working altogether. I tried calling friends. Acquaintances. Whoever. No one answered. It was almost a relief when it ceased to be an option."

Esther kept knitting.

"What about you?" Miranda asked. "Where were you?"

Esther seemed surprised that she asked.

"Me? Here in town. I had been working nights at the hospital. By the time I woke up and had some coffee and breakfast, it was all over. I came downtown and everyone was gone. It didn't look much different than it does now really. Except for the snow, of course."

"There were a few other people wandering about. A fellow who was a bit of mess. A bit touched. Covered with burn scars from some horrible accident. Something to do with drugs I think. He had a girlfriend or a wife. A tiny thing with thick glasses and thin hair who would follow him around, pushing her empty stroller ahead of her. They were both here. And the kids, the ones who were in school. Who had seen their teachers walk out the door."

Esther frowned and fell silent.

"So what did you do?" Miranda asked.

"What does it matter?" asked Esther. "What does it matter what I did? What does it matter what happened before? It doesn't matter at all. I shouldn't have asked you about it. It's none of my business, it's none of yours."

Miranda sat there for quite some time listening to the click-click-click of Esther's knitting. The needles kept flashing, the rows accumulating.

Mary was tiny, a fistful of bones and skin, no bigger than some small tragedy left behind in a nest, but she had a puckish smile and bright eyes that followed Miranda about the common room. Most of the time she spoke a German dialect that no one else could understand, but every once in a while she would manage a trill of clipped English.

Once, when Miranda was bundling herself up to go foraging, Mary said: "But there is no man to harness the horses to the sleigh."

Another time when Miranda was helping with the puzzle, she held up a little fragment of sky: "As blue as Rachel's pretty eyes."

Once, touching Miranda's cheek with her dry-as-dust hand: "Who will pray for you when I die?"

On one of her trips with Arthur, Miranda saw a thin stream of white smoke rising into the blue sky to the west. That evening while they were sorting her take, she asked Esther if it was the Mennonite.

"No," said Esther. "He lives over thirty miles away."

Miranda waited for Esther to offer more but finally had to ask, "Well, then who is it?"

"There are plenty of folks still in these parts. They keep to themselves."

"Like who?"

"Lots of folks," said Esther. "What's it matter who? They don't bother me and I don't bother them."

There were cats about. Dogs too, but not so many as to be a serious nuisance, and they knew better than to harass Esther. She had no qualms about shooting them. But the cats she put up with. There was a young orange one with a white paw that often came by. It would watch the chickens, feet together, tail wrapped tidily about itself. Joyce loved it, so if Miranda had a moment when the cat appeared, she would take the old woman out to see it.

Esther would be irritated, of course, at the commotion of bundling the old lady up in a coat and putting boots on her feet, and she would have been furious if she knew Miranda was smuggling scraps of meat out to feed it, but she couldn't begrudge Joyce a little happiness.

Miranda called it Buster and it would butt Joyce's hands fiercely, snaking in and out of her legs, tail trailing after it. Sometimes when Miranda was out with Arthur it would trot along parallel to them for a block or two, meowing plaintively, and Miranda would talk back.

"Going for a walk, Buster?"

"Looking for birds?"

"Looking for grub?"

Arthur would glare at it.

"They stink," Esther said one day when Miranda and Joyce came back in. "Horrible smell. Spraying everything. Disgusting."

"It's a female," said Miranda.

"If it has kittens on this property you're the one that's going to have deal with them."

"Give them treats, you mean? Bring them in for the old folks to cuddle?"

Esther snorted.

One night, Miranda woke up to howling dogs. She pulled on her clothes and went to peer out the windows of the common room. The howling stopped soon enough, but she grabbed the rifle Esther hung on a coat rack by the front door and went outside to check on the chickens. The birds were sound asleep in their little shack and there was no sign of the dogs, no footprints, no feces, no urine. It was cold and clear, the stars splashed against the night in their ancient constellations, a cold breeze washing down from the hills.

A light flickered in one of the windows on the fourth floor and a shiver swept across Miranda's skin. From neck to feet and back again. She recalled staring up at the Morgan Stanley Children's Hospital in New York at two or three in the morning, about a week after things changed, seeing a similar will-o'-wisp shimmer flitting from window to window. The city was largely deserted by then. Haunted by those ragged few remnants of humanity who hadn't streamed into the countryside to dig. That glimmer of light she saw in New York, that evidence of an entity like herself moving through the pitch-black hallways and wards, looking for something, perhaps for someone, had produced a burst of anxiety in her so intense she felt sick. Until that moment outside the hospital, she had not only avoided walking past the big institutions, but avoided thinking of them altogether; all those people helpless in hospital beds and jail cells slowly starving to death, blinded by darkness, dying of thirst, the prisoners in detention centers crying out for food, the chorus of their words disintegrating over time, disarticulating into the sound of pure despair.

She stood gazing at the faint light on the fourth floor of the apartment block for a couple of minutes, reliving that realization from the city, that awareness that hidden all around her were pockets of intense suffering; strange subjectivities existed trapped in impossible places; subjectivities weirdly similar to herself, but in situations of such misery she could barely imagine them, situations from which there was no possible escape but death.

The feeling passed as she stood there, listening to the wind in the trees. She felt the sweat cool on her brow as the memory of the hospital receded. Miranda went back into the building, returned the gun to its place in the lobby, and checked Esther's flat. The door was open and it was pitch black inside. She climbed up the stairs, feeling her way along the banister. The door at the top of the stairs was open, and she peered down the hall. Everything was quiet and dark. She padded down the hall until she found one door under which she could see the faintest glimmer of warm light. She listened intently but heard nothing. She returned to her bed and tried to go back to sleep.

She remembered a woman she met in Trenton who was walking up from D.C. to a prison in upstate New York where her brother was serving time for some meaningless crime. She remembered a man she had seen walking down the New Jersey turnpike, looking in every abandoned car, wordless with grim anticipation. She remembered breaking into her grandmother's house in suburban Philadelphia and finding it empty, aside from a layer of dust. It sat in perfect order: photographs of Miranda and her parents on the fridge, her aunt and uncles, a plate of cookies on the counter, two empty teacups, the pot in its cozy. What had she felt then? Was there a word for it? For the Russian roulette click of certain knowledge. Her grandmother joined the diggers in the fields somewhere and could never be found. Miranda could no longer be expected to look for her, to find her. Expected? Expected by whom? Was it relief, that strange feeling? Was it a species of grief? Of ecstasy?

She stayed two days at her grandmother's, sleeping on the couch, looking through photo albums, reconstructing her memories of childhood: road trips from the Midwest to visit relatives on the Eastern Seaboard, back and forth, back and forth; summer at the cottage on the Canadian border; Christmas mornings with her parents on the couch, smiling as she opened her presents, the wrappers on the floor, the smell of coffee and bacon; hockey on the radio in the garage as her dad puttered about; coming home from school once to find Mom weeping in the kitchen and never knowing why; visiting Gramma on her own for the first time and asking her all those questions about family stories, about her father's childhood, his youth, questions about her mother, trying to unpack the secrets of her origins. She went over those memories and many more besides, over and over, trying to make herself cry, but she could not. It all seemed arbitrary now, all those events and people, so disconnected from what her life had become, so entirely unrelated to her.

The ham was long gone when Esther shot a deer. It was a cold day and it came down from the hills to nose about in the parking lot snow for spilled grain. A couple of the old folk saw and went up to the windows to watch. Esther darted out of the room and a few minutes later appeared outside, flannel shirt thrown over her blouse, wool cap pulled down over her ears. The deer lifted its head and looked at her. Esther raised the rifle and shot it. It kicked out and leapt away, barreling into the bushes. Mary gasped. Arthur shouted. Esther slung the rifle over her shoulder and marched after it. Everybody went back to whatever it was they had been doing.

Miranda got herself together, collected some sharp knives and a heavier coat for Esther, and followed her out. The snow was stained with bright red blood and churned up by its flight. The deer did not get very far into the bush. Esther already had it on its back – legs splayed, head twisted on its long neck – and was running a hand over the pale fur of its underside. Miranda handed her a knife and she made a quick incision low down its belly and slipped her fingers under the skin to help guide the blade the rest of the way up to the sternum, the grey sack of the guts ballooning out as the animal was opened. Once it was dressed, they dragged it back home and strung it up in the basement laundry room.

Miranda went back out and piled the mess into a garbage bag and dragged it down the hill, dumping it out into a ditch. When she got back, Esther was outraged.

"You should have taken it farther or burned it. Now those dogs are going to be coming around."

Miranda went to wash her hands and Esther followed.

"You going to shoot any that come sniffing around my chickens?"

"Sure, I'll shoot them," said Miranda and poured meltwater into the sink.

"At least you could have mixed in some rat poison or something."

Miranda scrubbed at her nails with hospital soap.

"If they come up here and kill any chickens it's on your head," said Esther.

"Sure," said Miranda. "My head."

"So close to us. So close to the chickens."

Miranda kept scrubbing.

"Stupid," said Esther. "So stupid."

In the evening, as they were getting everyone ready for bed, they heard a dog fight down in the valley. Neither said a word until they were finished and Miranda went to the lobby to pull on her boots.

"Don't go," said Esther. She followed Miranda down the hall. "At least they won't be hungry, right?"

Miranda stopped lacing up and cocked her head.

"It's not so safe at night," said Esther. "Even if we both go."

About ten days after she killed the deer, Esther asked Miranda if she wanted to learn how to properly clean and butcher it. They went down into the basement with some bags to wrap the meat in. There was enough sunshine coming through the windows along the ground for Esther to work. The body of the deer was suspended hindquarters-down from a bare beam, head awkwardly bent to the side. Neither said a word, and their breath hung in the cool air like fog. Esther stared at the still body of the deer intently as she dismembered it, eyes dilated in the dim light, almost like she was reading a book or a newspaper, but to Miranda it seemed she proceeded primarily by touch, her hands reaching inside the ribs, feeling their way about secret topographies, following curves and swells, exploring hollows. The steel blade slipped through skin, fat, and muscle, and with gravity's aid, the creature was gently unknit from its frame, the waste piling up at their feet, Miranda wrapping up the good meat in the bags. When they were done, Miranda took the remains outside and burned them in an old drum.

That night, Esther made a venison stew with some red wine and cranberry jelly. The smell made everyone nearly delirious. Joyce hovered about, telling Esther about Uncle Reg ("always lock your bedroom door before you go to sleep," "he rattles the door handles in the middle of the night," "he was sad again yesterday, crying in the bathroom all afternoon, no one could get in and Sarah had to go next door to pee"); Mary and Betty sat up and sat down, moved from place to place, cried out petulantly, kept showing up at the kitchen door and impatiently staring in, eyes wide and mouths slightly open, Betty humming snatches of old pop songs and Mary whispering High German prayers; Jimmy sat at a table, gripping its edge, almost quivering with anticipation, occasionally wiping his wet lips dry with his sleeve; Arthur paced back and forth, back and forth, muttering and snorting.

The broth, when they finally got to it, stained their hands and mouths red.

After everyone was in bed, Miranda opened another bottle and drank it with Esther as they picked at the leftovers. And then another one which they half finished, before Esther, whom Miranda had never seen drunk, finally stumbled off to her apartment. Miranda took the bottle, went into the common room and collapsed into the reclining chair. She sat there and stared out the windows into the darkness. An almost-full moon lit the night sky and snow was scudding across the space between the building and the trees. The old folks were sleeping in their beds against the inside wall, dim piles of blankets, pillows, and sheets. A few were snoring. Miranda made a game out of guessing whose noise was whose: Arthur was the dry snuffle that built up into a throaty roar; Betty was the soft, wet whistle; Mary the mournful, fluttering hoot; Jimmy the stop-start hiccup of someone trying to rope-start an outboard. But Joyce was so ominously silent, Miranda eventually walked over and put a hand on the blankets to feel the gentle rise and fall of her breath. She went back to the chair, smiling at her anxiety, and fell asleep.

It was the cold that woke her from uneasy dreams, or maybe the heartburn. The moon was gone, and she could see nothing outside but the frozen night. The room was silent. She shivered, put the empty bottle away, and went off to find her bed.

Esther didn't come to check on her until lunchtime.

"A big storm blowing in," she said, handing Miranda a cup of instant coffee. "Better check on the nunnery."

"The nunnery?" Miranda croaked.

"Isn't that where nuns live? Isn't that what you call your chickens?" Esther said. "Nuns?"

The blizzard lasted two days, and on the first sunny day after it ended, Arthur lost his temper with the women working at the puzzle and beat Mary about the face so badly her eyes were swollen shut. They put Arthur in his own apartment. Mary lay in her bed for a long time, and then she died.

5

ANOTHER BIG STORM ROLLED in during what Esther said was March. Miranda wasn't convinced it was that late in the year, but Esther insisted – she was worried that the Mennonite had not come by. The drifts were so deep it took Miranda all morning to dig her way out of the nursing home to the chickens. It was very cold and the snow was light and dry. Sprays of it skittered about the crust that was forming on the surface and spilled into the trench as she worked. As she heated up, she discarded layers until she was down to a heavy sweater, jeans, mitts, boots, and a toque jammed on her head. She would pause occasionally to catch her breath and pinch the ice from her lashes. The sky was a cloudless blue. A long curving drift fell away down the hill towards Main Street, ice crystals glittering in the light of a sun that seemed to Miranda as small and hard as a ball bearing. Maybe three or four miles away, on the other side of town, a thin, twisting column of smoke rose.

When she was done, she stamped the rime from her boots in the lobby entrance, kicked them off, and changed her soggy socks before she stepped onto the clean interior floors. She found Esther kneading dough in the kitchen, forearms dusty with flour, face flushed from the effort.

Miranda peeled off her sweater, threw it over a chair, and put the kettle on the hob of the coal stove.

Esther pounded away, slapping and flipping the dough until it was smooth and elastic, lost in her labour.

After the water boiled, Miranda splashed some into the teapot, swirled it about and dumped it. She dropped a couple of teabags into the steaming interior, filled it up, and slipped a cozy over it.

Esther straightened up, blinking sweat out of her eyes and rubbing her forehead with the back of her hand.

"There's some smoke out there again," said Miranda, "to the northwest. Same place as last time."

"It's probably the kids," said Esther.

"What kids?"

"The ones at the mall," Esther said and attacked her dough again.

Miranda poured them each a cup of tea: one sugar for her, two for Esther and a spoonful of powdered milk. She took her cup in both hands and held it up to her face, inhaling deeply.

"What kids at the mall?" she asked.

Esther grimaced.

"Give me a minute," she said and divided the dough into two rough spheres. One she dropped into a bowl and covered with a dishtowel, the other she deposited into a Dutch oven. She wiped her hands on her apron and Miranda passed her the teacup.

Esther sipped at it noisily and sighed.

"There are some kids at the Blue Spruce Mall, on the way to the interstate. They've been there since the adults left. Maybe two dozen stayed behind, refused to follow. Less now, I'm sure."

"You don't have any dealings with them?"

"They don't much care for grownups. I knew a few of the older ones by name, but they're gone now. Hardly anyone left there who can remember the old days. When they reach puberty, the change comes and they wander off to find the others, to join the diggings. I used to bring them over food occasionally, but they didn't ever even thank me. Just stared at me until I left. Sometimes they sneak up here and raid the garden. But in the winter it's too far for them to come snooping, and like I said, they don't much care for adults, don't much seem to like us."

They sipped their tea.

"I think I'll hike over," said Miranda. "Maybe take them some venison."

"No," said Esther. "We need that meat."

"We can spare a few sausages."

"Winter is far from over and that Mennonite still hasn't come by. We don't know what we can spare."

"Fine," said Miranda. "But I think I'll go out there anyways to have a look."

"We have too much to do today," said Esther. "I wanted to wash the sheets."

"I'll go tomorrow then."

"It's bath day tomorrow."

A mist of snow was blowing in over the black hills, circulating over the apartment blocks, occasional intensities spinning earthwards in loose vortices. Drifts piled up over the abandoned vehicles in little hillocks like barrows. Miranda had acquired a pair of cross-country skis on one of her expeditions with Arthur and slashed down the slope from the nursing home at exhilarating speed, but in the town, wending her way between the humps and dips, it was harder work. The blank windows and dark storefronts made her think uneasily of funereal canyons and deserted crypts. Crows watched her from an apartment block rooftop as she passed by. When she turned westward, off the main drag, everything opened up to the sky again and her mood improved. She went skidding past half-buried strip malls and garages, hiked up a long residential street, skis at awkward angles, and looked back to admire her bird tracks in the snow.

Miranda heard the kids long before she saw them: a long trill of bright laughter followed by a burst of happy screams. She decided to approach cautiously, cutting across the parking lot of a car wash and then making her way through a stand of trees rather than going straight up the thoroughfare. The mall was on a hill and the kids were tobogganing: a motley collection of clumsy figures in red and blue and green and pink and purple toques and mitts and boots and coats and ski pants, they careened down the slopes on plastic sleds and inner tubes and cardboard boxes. Hours of play had cut out a few slick runs down the steepest parts, along which they would fly, shrieking, kicking up sparkling rooster tails when they overshot a turn and hit loose snow, toppling head over heels when they lost control over a hump, and when they survived the plummet they spun out onto the straightaway of the road, slowing into lazy diminishment, arms and legs akimbo, heads hanging back in post-ecstatic relaxation. Then they would trudge up the hill dragging their vehicles behind them, some daring to march right through the mad onrush of the other sledders, inviting catastrophic collisions and outbursts of hysterical laughter, others shyly skirting the chaos.

There were about fifteen of them, the youngest no less than eight, the oldest no more than twelve. Miranda crouched in the shadows and watched, reluctant to interfere in any way with their joy. Up and down they went, up and down, one or two or three drifting away now and then, to eat or pee or drink or whatever, before rejoining the carnival, up and down, up and down. Once there was a bad crash, knees catching chins, elbows flying, weeping and wailing, blood spat into the snow, but the sulk was brief.

It was late afternoon when Miranda arrived and the sun was already beginning to sink, but they showed no signs of slowing down. Her joints were cold and stiff and she was thinking of leaving when one of the children saw her. It was impossible to tell if it was a boy or a girl. The child, one of the smallest, gave the others a wide berth and was dragging a blue plastic sled up the hill. No more than twenty feet away, touched by Miranda's gaze, the child stopped and turned to look directly to her. They had a pinched face, sallow under the rosy cheeks, small, dark eyes like black stones.

They stared at each other for a second or two before Miranda backed away into the trees.

Betty continued to work at the puzzle by herself. Occasionally, Miranda would join her and help move pieces about the table. The image they were trying to recreate was a poster of ornate teapots. The frame was complete and the rest of the pieces organized into little clusters of similar color and texture. It was very slow going. Betty would turn each piece around and around numerous times before nudging it into matching shapes. Whenever she successfully put two together, she would smile and sit back to stare out the windows for a minute or two.

Joyce came over every so often to tell them about door handles rattling in the middle of the night.

Whenever Esther released Arthur from his apartment to mingle with the others, he glared at them. The snow was melting, so Miranda could no longer drag him about on her expeditions though town, and as a consequence he was getting increasingly bad-tempered. They kept an even closer eye on him than usual. He would shout at them for no reason. He heard slights and imagined insults from people who were barely aware of his existence.

"Don't do that!" he screamed at Jimmy one afternoon, when the other man fell asleep in the recliner.

Jimmy woke up grimacing in terror, scrabbling at the armrest.

"You have no right!"

Betty looked up from her work and Joyce scuttled away to her bed.

"You have no right!"

"Arthur!" Esther marched across the room and took him firmly by the elbow.

"He has no right!" he shouted and pointed a long bony finger at Jimmy. "No right at all!"

Jimmy started to cry.

"Arthur," said Esther. "You mustn't shout at Jimmy. You are frightening him. Can't you see you are frightening him?"

Arthur looked down at Jimmy in disgust.

"No right," he muttered. "No right at all."

Esther led Arthur away and Jimmy curled up awkwardly on his side and wept. Miranda sat on the armrest and rubbed his back until he subsided into silence.

The geese were flying north, streaming north really, in endless, mazy skeins. Miranda had never seen so many of them at once before. In such numbers they looked sloppy, out of synch. She broke into a house in a well-to-do development far north of her usual stomping grounds and found a wealth of pharmaceuticals and alcohol. She was sitting on the deck even though the wind was cold and wet, waiting for the Xanax to kick in while drinking a vodka tonic.

They were thriving, the geese and dogs and deer and rats. By the smell of it, cats too, and mice. There were plenty of mice in this house. They had been scuttling in and out of the basement for years, no respect for boundaries, for inside-outside, shitting everywhere, building nests in the couches and the beds. It was nice on the deck, though, seeing the new growth in the feral garden, green tendrils creeping up through the dead hand of the old vegetation.

Miranda thought about the kids at the Blue Spruce Mall. She imagined them curled up, snoring softly under heaps of blankets and sheets in a mattress store; sitting around a dead fountain playing cards, drinking scurvy Coke, and eating stale cereal by the handful. She imagined them in an unlit movie theatre, telling each other stories of the barely remembered past, acting out strange Oedipal myths about Mom and Dad on the narrow stage; making terrible sacrifices to pig-headed gods; terrified of puberty; terrified of the change that would descend. She thought of how few years they had to cram in so much fear. She imagined the child she had seen trudging up through the snow on the sledding hill. She imagined the child dying, curled up in the remains of winter, in a slurry of mud and slush, bony cheeks and knobbled elbows, legs bent with rickets, yellow teeth loose in red gums, eyes blank, impenetrable, flat.

"They don't like grownups," Esther had said, or words to that effect. "They don't much seem to like us."

And later, when Miranda returned from her expedition to the mall and again broached the subject of bringing some venison, maybe some eggs, maybe some stewed tomatoes out to the mall, Esther had been even more indignant, even more outraged, more hurt: "You don't get it, do you? They hate us. They hate us. They don't like us at all. Not one bit. They would rather die than have us help them. They don't trust us. They don't trust us."

"Why would they, I wonder?" Miranda asked herself. "Why would they?"

6

MIRANDA CAME HOME IN THE EARLY HOURS, before the sun rose. None of the candles were lit. Esther was usually up and busy by then. The halls and the rooms were void and dark and she clattered about in the lobby until she got a candle lantern lit. It painted the walls with orange and yellow, the shadows stretched and bent as she shone it about, splashing light over the chairs and the coffee tables. She felt like she was breaking into a tomb. In the main hallway the doors were all closed, the brass knobs glittering as she approached them. The door to Esther's apartment was open a crack, but there was no response to Miranda's calls. The remains of a supper were on the kitchen table and the sink was full of dishes. When she checked on the old folks she found Jimmy curled up and crying in his sleep again; Joyce stared out expectantly from the depths into the lamplight, eyes glittering, phosphorescent, listening for Uncle Reg. Betty had felt her way to the puzzle table and was sitting there patiently, awaiting illumination.

Miranda returned to the kitchen and started the coal stove, put on some water for tea and porridge, then went back into the main hall.

She could hear Arthur.

"Marigold!" he was shouting. "Marigold!"

He banged on the door, it boomed and echoed.

"Marigold!" he shouted.

"Just a second, Arthur!" Miranda hurried down the hallway. The key was in his door and she let him out. He was in his pajamas, the crotch and one leg stained black with urine.

"Marigold!" he shouted.

Miranda cleaned him up and brought him to the kitchen so she could keep an eye on him while she prepared breakfast. He was content to watch her work and even thanked her when she gave him a cup of sweet, milky tea.

Esther showed up as Miranda was dishing out the porridge in the common room. Her clothes were rumpled and her hair unkempt, eyes red, mouth pulled sharply down in the corners.

She stood in the doorway and watched Miranda work for a few seconds before she came to help.

The porridge was bland and creamy and slopped attractively into the bowls, a dollop of strawberry jam for sweetness dropped into the middle, where it slowly dissolved in the heat. Miranda liked to push it around and admire the wispy network of webbed pink-and-red traces it left in its wake.

"I thought you weren't coming back," said Esther.

Miranda said nothing.

"And that Mennonite has not showed up yet."

Esther sent Miranda on a bike to fetch coal from outside of town. Miranda spent the previous evening cleaning and oiling a bike Esther acquired from some specialty shop the previous summer. It was a beautiful machine, the wheels barely whispering as they spun, the gears switching so smoothly they sent shivers of pleasure up and down Miranda's spine. A bike trailer for pulling a child served as a wagon, thumping and bumping behind her as she sped through town, weaving in and out of the abandoned cars. Esther's directions took Miranda close to the mall where the kids had been tobogganing in the winter and she took a detour so she could roll right past it. The snow was long gone, the grass yellow and grey, still flattened, covered with trash: boxes, fluttering plastic bags, old shoes, tin cans and bottles, scattered pieces of clothing. There was no one about. No sound but the chattering of some birds and the wind whistling through the shattered windows of the nearby cars and the trucks.

Outside of town, the road wound out of the hills towards the interstate. The trees were not quite budding yet, but the air was mild and smelled of wet earth and decomposition. The rolling horizon was broken by a pair of massive cooling towers and a staggeringly tall brick chimney that loomed over the black trees, a behemoth rising slowly from its slumber.

The coal mine where she had been directed was barely visible from the road: rusted scaffolding, conveyer belts, corrugated steel silos, and various strange, anonymous functionalities. The place felt mystical and impenetrable. To Miranda the ruins were an echo of the complex asymmetries of the naked trees that half-obscured it. A great pile of tumbled coal, a small mountain of black fossilized decay, sat sucking up the light in the midst of all that chaos, a gift for the living from the gods of the dead.

Esther watched Miranda scrubbing the coal dust from her hands.

"It was a beautiful ride," Miranda said. "The road isn't too overgrown and you can really fly down it. I thought maybe I'd go explore the big power plant if you can spare me, and the weather stays good. Or keep going down that road, what's it called? Until I reach the Conemaugh."

"Black Lick Road," said Esther.

Miranda dried off her hands.

"Black Lick Road," she said. "I'm curious if there's still some digging going on down there. Isn't that where you said they went? To the Conemaugh?"

"What's it matter if they are there or not?" Esther was irritated.

"It doesn't," said Miranda. "I'm just curious."

Esther turned away and stared out the windows. Then she left the room.

It rained for a week. Miranda and Betty completed the puzzle and started a new one: sailboats. Esther spent more and more of her spare time in her room in the day, and more and more nights sneaking upstairs. Joyce wandered up and down the hallways trying all the locked doors. Arthur screamed at Jimmy every time he caught him napping.

"When do you put in the garden?" Miranda asked.

"It's too early," said Esther. "And the Mennonite promised me some seed potatoes."

"I can start digging it up."

"His wife was pregnant," said Esther. "Or at least the girl he liked to call his wife was."

They sat in silence, then Esther continued.

"She had Down Syndrome, always such a cheerful girl. And hardworking. He would bring her on his rounds and she would help me out in the kitchen when they spent the night. Rebecca he called her, so small to be pregnant, and so young."

One morning Esther did not show up for breakfast. Miranda got everything ready and everyone eating, then she went to look for her. She was not in her apartment. Miranda started up the stairs and met Esther coming down, bleary-eyed, hair a mess.

"Where are you going?" Esther asked.

"I was looking for you."

"Am I not allowed any privacy? A few hours off? You have to know where I am at all times?"

"I was a little worried."

"You have your trips into the wilderness. You have expeditions. Curiosity. You have your curiosity. Why shouldn't I have some time alone?"

"Of course you should," said Miranda.

"How often do you go up there?" asked Esther.

"Almost never," said Miranda. "But I know you do."

"Oh, you know? You know? You don't know a thing, not a damn thing."

Miranda said nothing.

"I'll not have you snooping around up there," said Esther. "It's none of your business."

"OK," said Miranda. "Sure."

"You are just a guest here after all," said Esther. "Just a guest."

Miranda heard the heavy equipment as she pedaled out onto the bridge. The land opened up below her for miles and she could see the Conemaugh meandering its way through the thickly wooded hills, green now, except where the diggers had cleared the banks of trees for a width of at least a half mile on both sides for as far as she could see. They were carving up the bare rock and earth into the usual curling, curving maze of deep trenches. The bridge was dizzyingly high and Miranda could barely make out the individual figures below, but the yellow and orange dozers and the land-movers and the dump trucks were easy to pick out, crawling about the black earth, churning up the mud and spewing black smoke. She walked over to the other side of the bridge and it was the same there, the works stretched on and on until, with the river, they turned and slipped out of sight.

She had seen much bigger works on the other side of the Appalachians, but it was still impressive, especially in such an isolated place. She wondered how many of them were living down there, how many survived the winters and the starvation and the plagues that periodically swept through the camps, she wondered how many had died and how far away the places were where they got their fuel and food, whether it came down from the Great Lakes or was shipped up from the south, she wondered how long before they would hook up with more diggings, to the north or the south, or whether they would dwindle away here, and die, and all their work would be reclaimed by the woods, their bodies lying where they fell, drying up or rotting away, devoured by dogs and bears and birds, scattered, consumed by the myriad of creeping, crawling things that lived on the forest floor, and whatever was left of them gradually transformed into mushrooms, and lichen, and mulch.

7

MIRANDA ENLARGED THE VEGETABLE PLOT. She turned over a couple of acres of clay in the flats below the nursing home and was clearing out all the saplings and brush that grew around it. She was thinking about digging up more of the rich earth, not entirely for the sheer pleasure of sinking the blade of the shovel into it, for the pleasure of feeling roots tear, of feeling the muscles along her spine and on her shoulders flex as she lifted out the clods of loam, but because she knew for once her initiative would not be a cause for complaint. Esther resigned herself to the fact that the Mennonite was not coming and was worried about their supplies of fresh food.

"He likely died," she said every day or two. "His seizures were getting worse. And now that poor girl all on her own."

The sunny side of the lobby became a plant nursery. Rows and rows of seedlings were growing in plastic trays and Jiffy pots Miranda found at the Lowe's near the mall. When she went out scavenging for them, she'd seen a couple of kids in the bush that was encroaching on the store parking lot but ignored them. She felt their goblin eyes on her as she cycled away with her take.

There was still a little frost at night but she was getting impatient to get the plants into the ground. She spent a lot of time fantasizing about fresh tomatoes in their tight skin, earthy carrots pulled up by the bunch, shiny peas rattling into a bowl as they were shelled. Esther insisted they wait to plant, that they shouldn't rush it. There was more frost to come.

She returned once to the diggings at the Conemaugh and cycled past, all the way to the interstate. A couple of tanker trucks bringing diesel for the diggings turned off the highway past her as she straddled her bike, the drivers glancing down at her from their heights. The trucks disappeared down a cracked old road into the woods, brake lights burning red in the shade. She listened to the rumble recede as they descended into the valley. She thought about following them to the encampment but instead pedaled out onto the main road. There were a few abandoned cars on the shoulder but towards the west, the center of the highway was cleared out by the big trucks.

On the way home she decided to visit the power plant but could only get the bicycle three-quarters of the way there. She hiked the rest of the way and climbed the fence into the overgrown grounds. The cooling towers were colossal, at least a hundred yards in diameter, serene and curved, and the brick chimneys seemed unfathomably tall. One in particular stretched higher and higher, up and up, on and on, brick upon brick, until, from Miranda's perspective at its base, it simply dwindled away into myth and fairy-tale. She broke into the interior and wandered around the hallways, exploring the machine rooms by candle-light, baffled by the shapes of things, by the dials and lights that shone like eyes, the shadows that leapt away into the deeper darkness as she approached. She was exploring the carcass of a giant sea creature, a primordial thing washed up from a time-lost ocean onto a twilight beach. When she went back outside, the white concrete cooling towers were the curved bones of Tiamat's skull; the chimneys were fragments of her ribs.

Miranda got up with the sun one morning and went fishing at a small dam about a half mile away from the nursing home. It was once surrounded by parkland, but now the woods were creeping steadily towards the shore, the roots of patchy bush reaching tentatively into the cool water, a rich green from the reflection of all the leaves. The little lake slopped lazily over the sloping holding wall and the falling water splashed prettily down the stone until it coalesced into a run at the foot of it and vanished into a gorge. She caught a couple of perch and cleaned them, throwing the guts into the trees. She made a small fire and cooked one of them on a stick, burning her fingertips as she picked the white flesh from the bones and tore off strips of crisped skin. She wrapped up the remaining fish in Saran and tucked it away. Esther would like it as a breakfast treat, fried up with a side of onions and potatoes.

When she got home she was irritated to find that Esther was not already working. Arthur was shouting for Marigold in his apartment and Jimmy was crying. She threw the perch on a cutting board and ran up the stairs. Sunlight was pouring into the hall through the window in the far wall, the air was swimming with dust motes. It was the fourth door on the left, slightly open.

"Esther," Miranda called and knocked.

"Esther?" she called and knocked again, louder this time.

The third time she peered in.

It was a tidily kept apartment: a TV in one corner with an African violet on it and spider fern beside, a few magazines arranged on the coffee table in front of the couch, the window with blinds up and the curtains open, looked out over town.

"Esther?" Miranda called again and entered. She could see into the kitchen, a few photographs on the fridge, a calendar on the wall. At the end of a short hall was the bedroom. The double bed was made but one side of it was somewhat creased, disturbed. There were some pictures displayed on the bedside table. Miranda walked in and looked at them: a picture of a middle-aged man in horn-rimmed glasses with sideburns and Esther's jaw; a family photo of the same man with his wife and two blonde daughters arranged around a picnic table sometime in the early Seventies; one photo of each daughter as an adult. In the larger of the two one of the women was posing with her own family in front of a mottled blue backdrop. The smaller was a portrait of Esther, maybe in her twenties, wearing a nurse's uniform, smiling broadly.

Miranda walked back into the hallway and paused at what was surely the bathroom door.

"Esther?" she knocked loudly. "Esther?"

She tried the handle. It swung open. Esther's appearance distorted by the few inches of water in which she had drowned, her face smeared, hips stretched out, breasts at her sides, hair a cloud of floating worms. Miranda thought of the Willendorf Venus. There were some empty pill bottles by the sink. And some clothes neatly folded and stacked on the toilet seat.

Miranda went to the living room and looked out the window. She could see the steeples rising out of the trees, the housetops in their rows beneath the canopy. She looked down and could see the tidy patch of earth she had turned for their garden; she could even make out the pattern of the shallow ditches she had scratched out with a hoe in preparation for planting.

It occurred to Miranda that Esther would have had to cart all that water up the stairs. She wondered how many trips it had taken.

II

THE ROAD

1

THE WHITE CERAMIC TILES that lined the tunnel glittered in the light of Miranda's bicycle helmet. Cars emerged out of the darkness like crystals, stalagmites, things growing but not alive. She peered into the interiors of vehicles as she pushed her bike between them, the beam illuminating the dusty contents. Everything seemed distorted by the weight of the earth and stone above her; the air thick and hard to breathe, the shadows compressed into viscous intensities. To stave off her growing anxiety she began to make a list of all the empty objects she had seen in the bright spring sunshine on the road to Pittsburgh: eggshells, tin cans, houses, insect husks, a cat skull, old boots, drainage ditches, eyeglass case, a purse, pill bottles.

When she got to "pill bottles" she found a car that wasn't empty: a child's remains were strapped into a booster seat in the back, soft-soled blue shoes still on its feet, skin like cured leather, blond hair shimmering in the white light. She continued on her way but no longer looked into the cars and spoke her game out loud instead of keeping it confined to her head.

"Dumpsters," she said: "Church parking lots, liquor bottles, cardboard boxes, adult video stores."

It was late evening so there was not a particularly startling transition when she stepped out of the tunnel onto the other side of the hill. But there was enough ambient light that she could make out the contours of the wooded valley the highway followed, even though the details were beginning to vanish in the shadows. She hopped on her bike and began a slow descent through the jumble of cars towards the city she knew was there. After a mile or so she came across the remains of an accident and a fire. She got off the bike carefully and picked her way through the burned-out ruins of cars and trucks. As the darkness intensified, she looked for a place to spend the night. She could catch glimpses of houses through the trees but she had a sharp headache and nausea and felt disinclined to leave the road. Eventually she found a semi cab and clambered into it. The cot in the back was neatly made. She lay down on it, and despite her throbbing head, fell asleep.

She woke up with the sunrise and crawled into the driver's seat to get her bearings. The highway followed the valley towards a pretty skyline. Bridges crisscrossed a sparkling river. Bulbs and spires of a large Orthodox church rose from the overgrown bush. On the far side all manner of industrial flotsam and jetsam lined the bank, and the buildings behind them disappeared into a wooded rise so steep you could almost call it a cliff. The road in front of her fell away toward a tangle of concrete overpasses and cement walls. She felt an echo of the anxiety she experienced in the tunnel at the prospect of entering the city. The thought of the narrow streets crammed with deserted vehicles, hedged in by glass and steel and stone, made her shiver. She drank tepid coffee from her thermos and ate cold chicken from the bone. She decided to follow the signs west across the river to the airport and avoid as much of the downtown as she could.

The vehicles afforded enough space that she could cycle easily through them. Her path was hedged in by cool concrete slabs and abutments. Weeds and scrub had not encroached far into this world and it felt calm and pleasingly inorganic. The pale sky seemed distant to her and there was no sound but the hum of her tires on the road and the occasional spurt of gravel. She chugged her way up a ramp onto the bottom half of a double-decker bridge. It was almost cold in the shade of that compressed space, with the breeze blowing through. She coasted to the edge and peered over, still on the bike, one hand against the siding. She could see the confluence of two rivers, a stadium and a ball park, green spaces consumed by vegetation, and a half-dozen iron bridges roughly suturing the banks together – yellow paint eaten away by rust. Barges and riverboats lined the river and in the distance she saw a submarine moored alongside the walkway, an old one, she thought, a veteran of the Cold War. She stood there for quite some time, listening to wind whisper through the abandoned cars.

When she got to the far end of the bridge she found it vanished under a huge slab of concrete into another tunnel. Miranda turned on her helmet lamp and pedaled into the shadows. A long time ago, someone had shattered the windows of all the cars. Shards of dust-covered glass filled their interiors. She tried to keep her eye on the light at the far end. The tunnel felt like it went on and on for miles and when she reached the end she gulped at the fresh cool air as if she had been holding her breath for the whole of her passage. Around her were steep slopes covered with a riot of green. Leaves hissed and fluttered in the breeze. The chatter of the songbirds was startling, nearly deafening after the silence of the city. She followed the road up a long curving rise, under a tall, teetering, rusting railroad bridge, and out into bright sunshine. The highway to the airport wound through the hills, past hotels and billboards and shopping malls, the cars lined up in both directions bumper-to-bumper, most with the doors left open by the drivers that deserted them. Miranda guessed they had all been walking away from the city, she imagined the endless stream of them, flowing like termites and ants into the open spaces, away from the concrete and the steel and the rock, toward places where the soft earth could be more easily turned. She rolled her bike onto the shoulder and followed their trail.

There was a rusting green sign that said the next exit was to

Moon. There were some dogs underneath it, nosing about in the underbrush until they heard her, looked up, and froze, ears up, tense. She loosed the handgun in its holster, watched them until they returned to their work and then she cycled away. Not too quickly, but at a faster pace than she traveled previously.

"Moon," she said to herself. "Dogs under the moon."

She saw the yellow and blue of the IKEA from the highway and on a whim decided to investigate. The parking lot was half-full of cars and the doors to the building open. She climbed the broad stairs from the dimly lit lobby up into the dusty darkness of the shop proper and wandered through it, lighting up the dioramas with the helmet lamp as she gazed at them, pausing to look at the display books clustered here and there like spider eggs. There was a preponderance of texts on mid-twentieth century American foreign policy. She found a collection of Susan Sontag's essays and popped it into her backpack. When she arrived at the beds, she threw herself on the largest one and reveled in it. She turned off the lamp and it felt like she was ensconced in velvet. She removed the helmet, shrugged off her backpack and the .22 and lay there in the annihilation of total darkness. She went over the day's events – the desolation of the city, the bridges and the tunnel, the raw silence of life – until she felt herself relaxing into blank meditation. After a minute or two images began to appear to her in random succession, visions saturated with color and detail, incoherent memories blooming with an almost unbearable efflorescence and then fading: a tiny, almost-decorative chapel in the grassy meridian of a divided highway; in her grandmother's apartment in Philadelphia working on a puzzle together – sliding the fragments of brightly colored sailboats about the table, the sensuous snap of two pieces locking together; in the backseat of her parents' car watching the rivulets of rain form and disperse on the window as they drove through a prairie storm; a late summer evening lying in bed, listening to the sound of the other children still playing in the street, luxuriating in sleepy boredom; shopping for clothes with her mom, the creak of the carousels turning, the hush-hush-click of hangers on their rods; opening a fridge in the middle of the night, the light spilling across the linoleum, the orderliness of the cartons and the jars and the Tupperware and downstairs in the basement the furnace wheezes into life.

She dreamed of bridges out of a city, the people streaming past the parked cars, thousands of them, tens of thousands, hundreds of thousands, all silent, all walking to the same destination. A child was crying, struggling against the tide, trying to go the other way, looking up into the faces, trying to find someone or something familiar. The walkers would brush past, not roughly but firmly, intent on their destination. Miranda was trying to calm the child, she tried to hold them still, she asked "What's your name?" The child kept tearing herself away, pawing at the walkers, but the walkers wouldn't stop.

She woke disoriented with an agonizing headache. She thought she was in her parents' house, her childhood house, waking up in the guest room, and she nearly called out for her father. She didn't understand why her head felt like it was cracking apart at the seams. The pain was so intense she was certain her skull would crack open and flood the world with blinding white light. As the agony subsided, she became more aware of her body, aware that she was lying on a comfortable surface, aware that she was clothed and wearing boots. Sensation slowly began to coalesce into a measured awareness of her situation, so that by the time she no longer felt agony but merely a dull, throbbing ache, she remembered exactly where she was. She lay still a few minutes more, feeling tears slick on her cheeks, feeling drained. Then she fumbled about for her helmet and flicked on the lamp. She looked around at the mausoleum in which she had been sleeping: all that dead desire and the strange forms into which it congealed. She could barely recognize the things she saw. Bookshelves, wardrobes, lamps, baskets – they were all arbitrary shapes to her, functionless, accidents of incomprehensible histories.

She sat up, tightened her laces, stood, slung her pack and rifle back on and trudged off into the depths of the store. As she left the bedroom section, she saw that the last bed there had also been slept in. The blankets were thrown back and the sheets discolored by rusty stains. Miranda bent closer, and in the blank white light of her helmet lamp saw pubic hairs in the linen, and what looked like crumbs. She touched the sheets but there was no noticeable warmth.

In office furniture she found a long coil of human excrement. It shone like petrified wood and when she poked it with the toe of her boot it fractured and split, crumbling into ash. She found some more in an aisle between perfectly geometrical wooden filing cabinets, at least a dozen ancient turds piled up like dead sea creatures and broken coral on the ocean bed.

Her exploration of the displays ended with steps down to the main floor and a vast, dark warehouse in which boxed goods were stacked in huge walls that formed long aisles. She thought of old-fashioned psychology, of an elderly Swiss man with round glasses in a tweed suit tamping down a pipe, she thought of Yeats hiding in his tower.

"The spiritus mundi," she said out loud. The words did not echo but fell at her feet.

She passed through the aisles which opened into a cavernous space like a stadium, and there, surging up from the concrete floor, was a massive statue someone had built from the disaggregated elements of all that carefully engineered North European design. The thing was a conglomeration of desks, bed frames, shelving, lamps and furniture, screwed together into a twisting spine that rose almost thirty feet into the air, a teetering skeleton of some monstrous lifeform, serpentine-segmented tentacles, long bent arms reaching out into the deep, dark corners of the room. She ran her hands over the lower portions, saw that it was not screwed together entirely with hex keys and wrenches but had been hammered, glued, tied, and even welded into a single mass, an organism with guts of tangled metal, wood, and taut rope ligaments.

The floor around it was covered with discarded boxes and she pushed some aside so she could wheel one of the warehouse stepladders near enough to clamber up and have a closer look. The top was not very different from the bottom: a chaos of repurposed parts that cohered together just enough that it seemed to her it must have some sort of specific meaning. But she could gather no sense from it as to the intent of the manufacturer, no sense of what that new purpose was, of what it signified, she had no way of knowing if it was finished, incomplete, in decay, or still growing. She understood nothing about it except that it was built by human hands.

It was early evening when she left the building. She spotted a single column of smoke rising into the sky, away from the highways, out in what she could only assume was the suburbs. She got on the bike and cycled back to the main drag, to the road west.

2

IT WAS IN A PRETTY LITTLE TOWN somewhere in northwestern Pennsylvania, not far from the Ohio border, where Miranda wrecked her bike. She was cruising by an old brick church and enjoying the turreted towers alongside its steeple, and the huge round windows that were not smashed yet, when she hit a pothole and went head over heels. She peeled the skin from her palms and jammed a shoulder. Her gear was strewn across the cracked road. She cleaned it all up before she looked at her bike. The front wheel was badly bent.

She sat on the church steps, picking the little stones out of her hand and washing the wounds with bottled water. Then she took a long drink. She did not think she could fix the wheel even with the proper tools. She thought about looking around the town for a bike shop. It was a clear, cool morning, an occasional breeze pushing her hair around. She admired the trees growing across the street and ate some cold beans left over from the night before. A crow watched her from a power line, head cocked, eye like a black stone. A Rockwellian billboard down the road in the direction she came from showed a small boy in overalls climbing a fence and declared that God knew her before he had formed her in the womb. She didn't really make a conscious choice, but after she finished eating Miranda stood up, swung her pack onto her back, and the .22, and hiked out of town, leaving the bike and its full trailer behind her.

The road climbed up out of the town, crossed a broad, shallow river and was soon a long, broad tarmac path curving through a forest of leaning trees and rough bush. She took the turnoff to Youngstown and found she was trailing after the old railway tracks and the river into an overgrown strip of industrial buildings, the brick and rusting metal slightly visible through the thick foliage. She realized she must be on one of the digger fuel arteries. The vehicles deserted here were pushed onto the shoulders or right into the weedy ditches. Soon she emerged out of the woods into a wide swath of worked land. It looked like it had once been good agricultural country, gentle and rolling, but now it was a network of massive dark grooves the diggers carved out of the heavy clay. With the bush cleared out, she could see the gleaming river, but the railroad tracks were buried under the earthwork. The far bank was still wooded. She kept walking until she came to a cloverleaf. She trudged up to the apex and looked around but it was not high enough to give her a particularly good view. She could see far enough to know it was a big dig, stretching for a miles in every direction, following the river as it meandered towards Lake Erie. There was some movement far to the southwest of her: dust, and the sun glinting off metal. She could hear the faint bass rumble of big diesel engines.

She kept heading for Youngstown. By early afternoon she reached the state line and dug around in a dollar store for food. She found cans of black-eyed peas and tinned ham. She lit a fire in the parking lot and while the food heated, she dragged out a reclining lawn chair. After her lunch, she lay back on the chair and fell asleep in the sun.

It was the sound of the motor that woke her up, but she was

so distracted by the throbbing pain in her jammed shoulder she didn't react as quickly as she should have. When she did finally sit up the vehicle was already there. It wasn't a digger truck but a white van hauling a fuel tank. It slowed down as it approached and then swung onto the lot, the gravel growling under its wheels. Miranda stood up. She didn't reach for the .22 but rested her hands on her hips near the .45.

The door swung open and a man stepped out: a black man, tall, thin, carefully groomed hair turning grey, goatee, leather shoes, leather jacket and a silk shirt tucked into a broad belt, unarmed.

"Hey," he said. "It's a beautiful day."

Miranda said nothing so he strode over and stuck out a hand.

"Dave," he said.

Miranda watched him warily.

He let the hand drop and grinned.

"Anyways. A beautiful day. Always a beautiful day when I meet a fellow traveler."

He looked around.

"This your place?" he asked.

She shook her head.

"Mind if I have a look around? Mind if I see if there's anything worth appropriating in there?"

Miranda shrugged. While he was inside the store, she kicked out her fire and gathered up her gear. The pack's weight made her damaged shoulder burn. She strode off.

He caught up with her about a half hour across the state line. She heard him coming and turned to watch his approach. He came to a stop beside her and leaned toward the window so she could see his face.

"Look," he said. "I understand if you aren't interested, but we're going in the same direction, right?"

Miranda stared at him and tried to ignore the throbbing in her shoulder.

"Well, we are," he said.

Miranda said nothing.

"And I'm bored and lonely and sometimes even silent company is better than none. I'll give you a lift as far as you want, I won't be insulted if you keep that gun handy, keep it right out on your lap if you want. Totally fine with me."

Miranda shook her head.

"Ok," said Dave. "I'm going as far as Youngstown today. I'll be camped on the outskirts and grilling some pork. Fresh pork. I shot a pig outside of Butler. I'll make sure I'm somewhere where you can see me. You can join me if you want."

She smelled his camp before she saw him: wood smoke, melting pig fat, and weed. He was parked outside an old barbershop and sitting on a camping chair, a bottle of wine between his legs, having a long pull on a doobie while he watched the sun set over the desolation of the rust belt. A tightly covered aluminum tray was sitting in the charcoal and a cooler beside him. Her shoulder was aching, her hands stinging, and her stomach empty of everything but acid.

When he saw her, watching from the road, he went into the van and dug out another chair for her, set it up, and went back to his own seat. When she came over and sat down he handed her the doobie without a word and she had a couple of puffs.

"Wine?" he asked and she shook her head.

After about half an hour, the sun set and he peeled the foil from the aluminum pan. The outside of the pork shoulder was charred and when he stuck a fork into it, the meat fell apart into fat buttery chunks. He piled up a pair of paper plates with meat and poured her some wine. This time she did not refuse.

"So many pigs," Dave said as he ate. "So many pigs running around America. Maybe not so many up here but you should see what it's like in North Carolina. I swear someone down there went from farm to farm opening all the gates and they all ran free. Thousands. Hundreds of thousands. Millions. Lots of chickens too. It's a paradise of sorts. Sleep out of doors. Shoot a pig whenever you're hungry. Because we're never going to run out of bullets either, are we? Pigs and bullets, that's our patrimony, feral pigs, endless bullets, and baseball caps. Have you ever stopped to think how many baseball caps are out there? In the stores and in the homes. We'll never run out. Our inheritance. The never-ending bounty of our civilization. And mattresses. Pigs, bullets, baseball caps, mattresses."

"Tampons," said Miranda.

Dave laughed.

"Yeah, lots of tampons too, they left us all the tampons too," he said. "I guess the list goes on and on. I was beginning to think you were mute."

Miranda shook her head. The wine was a lovely mellow red.

"Have another plate of pork," Dave said, but she was worried too much of the fatty meat might make her sick.

"Where you headed?" he asked and she shrugged.

"Well, west anyways," he said. "You're walking west and I'm going west too. Want to see the Great Plains before I die. And the Rockies. Maybe even the Pacific Ocean. Wouldn't mind finding a pharmacist as well, a chemist, a guy I know told me a guy he knew said there was a chemist at the University of Chicago, in the labs, and he could make you up anything you might want. Anything! That's the Holy Grail now, isn't it? The new alchemy, someone who can make drugs out of the leftovers."

A spasm ran up his neck and across his cheek. He took a long pull on his joint.

"This self-medication can only do so much for a guy," he said. "Speaking of which, I got pills if you want any. Oxy? Codeine? Ritalin?"

"I'm OK," said Miranda. "Listen, thanks for the food and the wine, it was fantastic, but I should probably find somewhere to sleep."

"Well," said Dave. "Go ahead. Lots of housing around here. And I haven't seen anyone about. But feel free to stay by the fire or sleep in the van."

"I should go find my own place," said Miranda, although she didn't want to leave her chair, leave the warmth and the light, and the company.

"Alright," said Dave. "If you want to tag along, come by in the morning. And I'll leave you the pork if you don't show up."

"Thanks again," said Miranda and stood up. "I mean it. Thanks."

"No problem," said Dave and shouted after her as she trudged away: "Nice to have someone to share it with!"

She stopped when she got out into the darkness and looked back. He was in the circle of the fire, feet up on the cooler, wine bottle back between his legs, rolling another joint. There were plenty of houses about, lots of cheap housing. Project housing. Poor folk once lived here. She went into the first place she found with an open door, collapsed into a dusty-smelling bed and fell asleep.

In the morning, her shoulder was so sore she could barely lift her pack and the scabs on her hand were split open. She set out and discovered her knee was also raw and stiff. Dave had already packed up when she got to the barbershop and was staring out across Youngstown, at the mist drifting through the treetops, and the office blocks shining in the sun, at a football stadium rising out of the landscape like the corpse of a mammoth emerging from the tundral thaw. An aluminum tray of shredded pork, a bottle of wine and a Ziploc bag packed tight with weed were waiting for her by the ashes of the fire.

3

MIRANDA WAS DOING ALL THE DRIVING because Dave kept getting little seizures and putting the van in the ditch. He called them popcorn seizures and swore up and down he could usually simply grit his teeth and fight through them but after it happened twice in one day, and then again first thing on the next, Miranda kicked him out from behind the wheel and took the keys away.

"I've been unmanned," Dave said. "Emasculated. Dehumanized."

But he did not seem to be too upset about sitting in the passenger seat rolling joints with his long fingers, telling her what he knew about the history of these parts, the olden times, the three-cornered hat days, about the white settlers swarming over the Appalachians in the years after the Revolution, and the massacres and the swindling and the bloodshed. And he told her all his various theories about what it was that was happening to humanity now: "the future times," he called it, but what he meant was clearly this time around. He told her about transhumanism and posthumanism and something he called the pharmo-genetic singularity, which led to their present predicament: viruses, mutations, uncontrollable chaotic change only now settling down into a new pattern. Lots of theories Dave had, lots of theories.

It was nice to listen to his voice and drive, elbow out the window, wind in her hair, shifting up and down through the rolling country, watching the turkey buzzards circling and the geese flying north, keeping an eye on the precious trailer of fuel in the rear-view as it jockeyed about behind them, watching it creep closer on the down slopes, and slip back on the ups. It had taken them half a day to pick their way through Youngstown. The streets were crowded with ditched vehicles, and even when they were free from the urban congestion, they had to weave slowly northwards through the static traffic. It was late afternoon on the second day when they reached the big east-west highway. Dave said it was cleared of deserted vehicles so the diggers could haul diesel from the ports in Toledo and Cleveland to the big digs that were running all along the south shore of Erie and up into the northern Appalachians. They hadn't seen any of those tankers yet, but Dave was sure they were coming now that spring had broken the back of the long, cold winter.

"Some of those people up around Scranton didn't fare so well," he said. "The diggers, I mean, not the folks like us, not the regulars. Those diggers were all cheekbones and loose skin and big, sad eyes. They'd hear me coming and wander out of the trees in the hope that I was fresh supplies. But what could I do?

There were too many. The first time I stopped and handed out some granola bars and gave them a couple of pounds of flour, but really, I needed that stuff for myself, not just to eat, but for trade as well. And they didn't have any fuel. So it was false charity, you know, just a grotesque performance we were indulging in that didn't improve my feelings, their situation, or my feelings about their situation, it didn't really improve anything at all, not really. Probably all dead by now, dust and bones, but still, never a word out of them, just those staring eyes, blank eyes, never a 'thanks,' never a chance for me to say 'no problem, you're welcome' and feel pious for an hour or so. They only take what you give them, that lot, and walk away."

"Ungrateful bastards," said Miranda wryly but she felt sick. She thought of Joyce and Betty and Jimmy and Arthur, what would have happened to them by now, what they will have become, how their histories will have merged with those of the Scranton diggers.

Dave laughed.

"What do they think?" he said. "Do they think that shit just stole itself?"

The highway they were on was raised and they had a view of the wooded hills and overgrown farms rolling off in every direction until in the far distance they evaporated into haze.

"These huge concrete bridges," said Dave. "They always put me in mind of colossal skeletons, the arched spines of long-dead monsters protruding out of the earth. I imagine archeological digs laying them bare. Or paleontological? Anyways. No difference now. That's how I imagine these things, as things previously underground, buried, only recently emerging, set free by the wind, by the weather, by erosion."

"What about the cities?" asked Miranda. "How do you imagine them?"

"Shattered ribs. Massive teeth. Leviathan's corpse."

The sun was in their eyes.

"Strange cement accretions," Dave said. "Corals built up over the centuries, the microscopic creatures that once lived in them dead and now their shells are home to strange new creatures. Not animals: forces. We have been replaced by forces incomprehensible and barely visible. Luminous clouds drifting through the streets and the boulevards and the alleys like jellyfish, the long eel of the wind slipping in and out of shattered windows, the inhuman weight of history, deep oceanic pressures, we're at the bottom of the Marianas now."

He lapsed back into silence. Miranda could hear the engine doing its work, the air whipping around the car. She felt the highway through the tires, through rubber and steel, the swells and dips of the land beneath her like waves, was aware of the scrubby overgrown land falling away from them to the north, drifting away until it sunk beneath the grey undulations of Lake Erie. It was a kind of echo, the road, a repetition of that coastline, of the flattened parabola of boulders and muddy beaches and gnarled thirsty roots.

Dave dug around in the glove compartment and pulled out a few dog-eared notebooks in a muted rainbow of colors and a pen. He selected the green one and began writing in it.

Dave was staring out the window to the north and the sun was even lower now, getting fat and orange on the horizon, and the wheels were humming with the electricity of the road.

"Up here," Dave said. "There's a truck stop up here. Pull in here."

There were a good twenty trucks in the parking lot, looking broken and crooked but probably all fine. Dave rifled through five or six of them before he found what he was looking for: a little baggie of brown powder in a glove compartment. There were some picnic tables in the back of the place and they broke one of them up and got a roaring fire going. The sun had set but the crowns of the black trees that surrounded them were stained red. The western sky was a wash of lemon and pearl but up above it was already an oil spill. Miranda wrapped a blanket around herself while she watched Dave go to work, boiling water and cooking his heroin over a candle. She was smoking a skinny joint he had passed to her, he called it a pinner, and drinking a fifty-dollar Beaujolais straight out of the bottle.

"That's my favorite thing about the whole post-apocalyptic scenario," said Dave as he drew up the drug into his needle. "That's what I always looked forward to, access to all that fine liquor."

"Not the polygamy? I thought that was always the dream, all that self-righteous spawning."

"Oh God, no," said Dave while he clenched and unclenched his fist. "Rebooting humanity. Starting over. Who would want that kind of pressure? All that heartbreak? Just the wine, thanks. And all the leftover pharmaceuticals."

He tapped the syringe.

"Humanity," he said. "I like people OK, I suppose, but really, they expect so much from a guy. Conversation. Questions. Mutual interest. Always handing the words back and forth. Making up the sentences. Expecting you to say what you're thinking even when you're not thinking anything at all. All that thinking about what to think and then all that thinking about what to say. What not to. Words, words, words: back and forth, back and forth. I like a bit of silence."

"You've barely shut up since we left Youngstown."

"But that's just it. It's not thinking at all, what I just called thinking, it's a nervous twitch, all this talking, a spasm, a type of unconscious electrical discharge more than conversation, just snapping and cracking and popping. Static. The things I say have virtually nothing to do with what I'm actually thinking, let alone feeling, and who knows what they have to do with the unconscious processes that make me do the shit I do. I certainly don't. Words are camouflage, sleight of hand, an entertaining distraction so you don't notice the things that matter, the dangerous things, vulnerable things. I'm simply an octopus trying to hide, mottling along the ocean floor, squirting clouds of devious ink in my wake, waiting for a chance to squeeze my placental self into some crevice or another, where I will palpitate nervously until you get bored and go away."

He tapped the syringe again.

"You want to get high?" he asked

"No, thanks."

"Good girl," he said. "Enjoy what little of reality you got left to you, what little of life."

"What about you? What about your little bit of life?"

"Me?" He drawled. His veins were long, thin fingers crawling up the hard muscle under his skin. "All I got left is my curiosity."

He slipped the needle in.

"If I wasn't so goddam curious I would have ended it all right after it happened, you know? In the first few days. When my wife wandered off. And then my kids died, you know, one after the other, real quick. And it wasn't my fault, I don't think, but still, I'd-a killed myself then, I think, but I was so curious."

He slowly depressed the plunger.

"So goddam curious. What happened? What is happening now? Why? What's going to happen next? What are folks going to do? The rest of us, I mean. What are they going to say or do? Who can possibly imagine? Who can guess? I was always a pessimist I think, even before, but curiosity kept me going. Everything is so interesting, even when it's shit. Since long before, that's how I was. Always thought it would end badly, but couldn't stop paying attention. Everything I did. My life. Relationships. Everything people did. The world. It horrified me all along. But in a way, that made me want more of it. Life was a sort of a scab I couldn't stop myself from picking at. Or my thoughts, rather, were a sort of a scab I wouldn't let close over my mind. Just kept picking at them with questions. Pointless questions. They did nothing but keep me raw. Keep me irritated. Angry."

He pulled the needle out and laid it on the picnic table.

"What did you do before?" Miranda asked.

"Me?" He was pressing a cotton swab against his arm.

Miranda nodded.

"Before?"

"Before all this shit happened."

"I was a union organizer," he said. "Down south. Those farm workers down there. Sí, se puede."

He closed his eyes and leaned back.

"Those truckers," he sighed. "You can always count on those motherfuckers. Sí, se puede."

4

THE LAND ON EITHER SIDE of the highway was stripped bare, turned over, and carved up into a wasteland of twenty-foot deep, curving, curling channels. Miranda pulled over onto the shoulder to get a closer look. She stepped out of the vehicle and the wind whipped her hair around her face. There was a red-winged blackbird on a slack telephone cable squalling away and a clutch of pussy willows growing out of the drainage ditch. She scrambled down into the ditch, hopping across the scummy water, and scrabbling up the other side out over a tumble of dark clay. One of the giant grooves opened up right in front of her, a yawning throat falling away in a steep slope until it leveled out into shadow.

She glanced back at Dave. The passenger door was open and he had one leg resting on the gravel, the other tucked away inside. He shrugged.

She walked down the slope into the maze.

"Don't get lost in there," he shouted but his voice sounded thin and unimportant.

Up close the walls that seemed so smooth from the road proved to be winding, crumbling barrows of piled clay, mud, and sand. The fifteen-foot wide floor that ran between them was a patchy jumble of inorganic patterns: the dozers' treads left a tangle of beetle-humped tracks, and their giant steel trowels sheared great triangular slices out of the floor and walls, massive wheels churned up the heavy mud into half-moon banks and left glimmering black lagoons in their wakes. Hairy, old roots reached out from the sides, dead fingers from the mortuary earth. Stones – a million grey-and-white teeth—protruded from the soil. It smelled moist and felt still in the trench but up top it was a dry windy day, and a scuttling breeze spilled sprays of dirt over the edge and chased spinning, spitting vortices of dust across the face of the distant blue sky. It was cold out of the sunlight and Miranda shivered. She followed the twists and turns for a quarter of a mile or so until she reached what could be called a crossroad, where her groove intersected another. She stopped there for some time, thinking about the immensity of the labyrinth she was in: it extended for at least a mile on either side of the highway, and they had been driving through it for a good fifteen minutes before she stopped to have a look. It was the biggest of the works she had ever seen but Dave seemed unimpressed. And she had certainly heard of bigger. Still, she felt a surge of claustrophobic panic at the thought of all those endless, open tunnels, lost in the catacombs, a fly in the web. She stared up at the sky. It was icy blue and vacant, even though she knew it was spring up there, that on the surface the air was warm, filled with pollen and bees and butterflies and birds, filled with buzzing and humming and chirping, she knew things were blooming and budding, melting, decomposing, stinking, the shroud of all those frozen months was unraveling. She wondered if Dave would be irritated at how long she was gone, how far she had wandered. She wondered if he would be worried.

When she got back to the van low hazy clouds were blowing in from the west and a dust devil was shimmying across the road. The wind was intensifying. Dave had closed the door and fallen asleep against the window. She got in and closed the door gently behind her. He woke up briefly when the engine wheezed to life but simply blinked at her a couple of times and rolled back over, burying his face in the seat.

Soon sand skittered across the cracked pavement in shifting parabolas, the blue sky was stained mildew and rust, the sharp corrugation of the trenches softened by long, smeary tails of blowing dust.

Later, when Dave woke, he said: "For a while I imagined them as the grooves of a record, you know? Those old vinyl records. I thought, what if they contained information like those records did, and the wind was the needle. I thought, what if when they were all complete the wind would rush through them, oohing and ahhhing, moaning and groaning, building up a, what do you call it? A resonance? A harmonic resonance? That feedback deal like what happened to that bridge in Washington."

"Tacoma Narrows," said Miranda.

"Yeah. Tacoma Narrows. What if the wind would rush through them, through the grooves, and the sound waves or what have you would reach some kind of critical frequency and the earth, you know, would finally speak, you know? In undulating vibra-tions. Finally sing. The unconscious earth. The sleeping earth would finally wake. And the singing. How would it sound? How would the earth music sound? Like the angels and the whales? Like trees creaking? Like the surf? Like all those half-heard canyon songs and gully songs, and the rushing air whistling through the empty cities, through the alleys and the streets and the avenues and roaring across the barren industrial wastes and the railyards with the rattling cars? Imagine all that wind, the entire rushing atmosphere that weighs so heavily on every-thing, boiling under its own weight, sinking turbulent into these channels, concentrated, narrowed, intensified into a luminous, searing, shining noise, a volcano of noise, a geyser, a shattering anti-hallelujah chorus of impossible magnitude. A big noise, anyways. A big noise. And maybe, to us, this wind, this massive compression of air into the grooves, cold air warming up, heat-ing up, pressure-cooking, becoming molten, blowing its white-hot shrieking steam whistle heat through the narrow channels would be a demonic scream, a deafening, destroying, annihi-lating, eternal, endless, and irrevocable feedback roar. Imagine that: a noise that destroys all life. A song. A melody. A horrific melody.

"And imagine one day millions of years after we're all dead and gone, imagine aliens land here, millions of years from now, on this empty, be-grooved, shrieking planet. And they listen and they hear that song and to them, to their advanced cognitive systems or whatever, the unholy blast, the blast that is from us, and destroyed us, to them it is divine and beautiful and illuminating, it solves all their problems, all their anxieties, their chrysalis miseries, and they bloom, they grow, they transform into what intelligence is supposed to be, what we wanted to be, what we could have been, if we were better, more developed, or advanced, or whatever the word is now, what if it could have been the sound that released our better halves, instead of being the sound that ensured the destruction of our worst, but it won't matter then, of course, because our bones will be long gone, our own grooved brains melted away, decomposed and disintegrated, subsumed into the dust, subsumed into the dust, into the record's grooves, the recording grooves, and we will just be an infinitesimal part of the friction that makes the air sing, the white-hot friction that makes the planet sing. How's that for a story? Hey? That was my theory for quite some time, a month or two, the grooves were a means of containing and communicating information, data, not music, not really, but something, information, who knows about what, or for whom, or what it has to do with us.

"What reminded me of that theory, just now, was the sight of all that sublimating dust, all that decay and degradation, all that labour disintegrating, all that data blowing away. Not a good medium really, dirt. When the vehicle for communication, for unpacking the information, the wind, is, you know, when it is also the means by which the data is corrupted, by which the information is destroyed, that isn't so good, it suggests a design flaw."

They were pulled up on the shoulder waiting for the dust storm to end when the tanker trucks came careening out of the orange smog of blowing sand and dirt: dark, rumbling behemoths with burning eyes and shimmering double-jointed silver tails, breaching, filling up the world with spinning wheels and whistling steel and the diesel stink of hell and then vanishing just as quickly into the golden void, one after the other. Dave counted them, made observations, wrote numbers down in his notebooks.

They woke up when the storm had blown itself out. They were groggy, uncertain if the convoy was real or a dream, or something else. The sun was still high and the landscape looked untouched. Miranda started the motor and they continued their journey, reaching the edge of the digging without either of them saying a word. The chaos of the bush after all that barren raw soil was a relief, but the trees did not cover the land here as thickly as before, and the hills flattened out into gentle swells in which you could now see the old structure of the farms and the gas stations and the roadside picnic stops, badly set bones showing through soft skin. About an hour into this new land-scape, they came across a series of road signs that were painted over with the words: Fuel. For. Trade. Next. Right.

"Let's check it out," said Dave.

"But the trailer tank is half full," said Miranda.

"Got to take your chances when you get them," said Dave.

So Miranda swung off the highway at the next right and drove slowly down a cracked and weedy road that ran through a long stretch of burnt-out gas stations and fast food restaurants. The signs here were painted over as well: Fuel. For. Trade. Fuel. For. Trade. Fuel. For. Trade.

After a couple of minutes, a big arrow painted on a stained cardboard sign directed them down a side road that was little more than a double furrow through overgrown cornfields. They drove half a mile until their way was blocked by a closed gate. A sign hung on it: Fuel For Trade. Beyond the gate the fields ended and evergreens crowded the road.

Dave hopped out and opened the gate. Miranda eased the van and the trailer through the gap and Dave closed it behind them.

5

THEY WERE SITTING AROUND a roaring fire eating BBQ pork from paper plates, smoking weed from Dave's big sack, and drinking lukewarm vodka from brittle plastic cups. Miranda was drinking a lot less than Dave but even for her things were already a little unstable, the ground shifting about when she got up to go for a pee, the stars sliding about as she stared at them.

The three men were laughing at Dave's stories. They were laughing at their own stories too, but Miranda didn't much care for their stories. She didn't think they were funny. They were all smashed, the three men and Dave. The three men disclosed that they regularly robbed the digger convoys as they drove up and down the highway, and had accumulated a big store of food and diesel. They would park a semi across the road and when a digger truck pulled up, they would drag the driver out, and make him stand there and watch while they stole his fuel or his sacks of beans and salt pork or what have you. All they lacked was drugs, and Dave was going to set them up pretty good for those now too.

"Those dumb fuckers never say a word," the one they called Smacksburg said. "They stand there and watch us take whatever we want. Just stare into space."

"Fucking zombies," the big blond guy with the dead eyes and the gingery beard spat into the fire. His name was Evan. "Cattle. Fucking steer."

"You know they don't fuck, right?" said Smacksburg and glanced at Miranda.

"What's that?" Dave lit up another big fat Bob Marley joint.

"They don't fuck," said Smacksburg and glanced at Miranda again. "They're celibate. Like monks."

"Fucking steer," said Evan.

"How do you know?" asked Dave.

"I been watching them pretty close for a while now," said Smacksburg. "I'm not freaked out by them like some people. Sometimes I go right into the camps and wander around, checking things out, eating their food, taking shit."

"That's not all you do," muttered Evan.

The third man was skinny, more tattered and ragged and run-down than the other two. And unresponsive. He ignored Dave's questions entirely and didn't interact with his companions. Miranda watched him as she ate, only half listening to the others. The pork was dripping with fat, cut with a sharp spike of vinegar, and saturated with smoke. In the first few weeks in New York, after things changed but before she left for Philadelphia to try to find her Gramma, it seemed like the whole world was populated with people who resembled this third man, looked like they were barely clinging to reality. She felt hurt it was just her and them, her and the schizophrenics, the disturbed and the unstable. Everyone else had abandoned them, abandoned her, crossed an invisible barrier to some other unimaginable world. Now she found herself admiring him, admiring his self-containment. He gave nothing away, he did not care what these other men thought, did not care about the outcome of their arguments, about how their ideas differed from his. He ate his pork. He drank his vodka. He thought his own thoughts.

"But I've seen babies in those camps," said Dave. "And young kids. Not many, but some."

"I'm telling you," said Smacksburg. "They don't fuck."

"But Smacksburg does," sneered Evan. "Don't he, Smacksburg?"

That was when Miranda went for a pee. When she was done, she wandered past the laughing men in their circle of flickering light and stood in the darkness looking down on the little lake. The men occupied some kind of old government garage with a row of raised gas tanks now filled with stolen fuel. A bulldozer and a semi cab were parked in front of a utilitarian concrete block and a couple of old cars in various states of deconstruction were scattered about. The pine trees grew next to the sprawling yard on three sides. On the fourth, a meadow sloped down to the water. When Dave and Miranda rolled onto the lot, the three men had been standing at the top of the meadow,

Evan carrying an automatic rifle. Past the men, Miranda spied a caravan parked on the shore, not one of those sleek, curved containers she would have liked, but an ugly tan box with a door and some windows cut into it. Now, in the night, the caravan was simply a patch of impenetrable darkness against the glittering black water.

"Where'd you find him?" Evan was standing at her shoulder.

"He found me," said Miranda: "Just north of Pittsburgh. I'd crashed my bike and was limping along on foot when he came steaming up the road and offered me a lift."

"Don't see many black folks around here anymore," said Evan. "Especially not black men with white ladies."

Miranda ignored him.

"So where is he giving you this ride to?"

"He's going out west, Chicago, but I'm not stopping there. I had some people up in Minnesota I want to look in on."

"They'll be dead or digging."

"Yes," said Miranda and turned to go back to the fire.

"So then what's the point of all that travel?"

"I don't suppose there really is a point," said Miranda. "But it's what I decided to do. Just like you guys decided to camp out here, rob convoys, and get high."

"That's right," said Evan. "That's the future we chose. Why choose disappointment when you can choose this? When you can have all of this?"

She returned to the fire and tipped back a mouthful of vodka. It tasted like acetone. So she had another. Dave kept rolling joints and passing them around. Miranda was very high. She heard the words that followed the weed around and around the fire, but she couldn't concentrate on them long enough to string them together into sentences.

Smacksburg was still talking about the diggers. His bearded mouth was a hole in the ground, moist and dark, a fresh grave full of worms, his eyes were worms, his words were worms.

"They never talk," said Smacksburg and Miranda frowned at his words. "Never. They've gone dumb. It's like they went backwards, like they're animals. Regressed."

"They aren't animals," said Dave, and she swung her head heavily to see him, to see him lean in earnestly towards the other man.

"They don't talk," said Smacksburg. "They don't take care of their kids, they don't love each other, they don't plant food or hunt or anything, they dig up the fucking ground like fucking voles, or gophers or lemmings or something, and if the food doesn't arrive in time they just lie down and die."

Miranda was aware she could get up and walk away from the conversation. She could stand up and go sleep in the van. She could stand up and walk into the darkness, retrace her steps to the highway, spend the night in a gas station and then keep walking west in the morning. She needed nothing from any of these men, but she was drunk and tired and stoned and wanted to lie down somewhere warm and close her eyes.

"They communicate somehow," said Dave. "Those trucks roll across the landscape pretty regularly, those camps are organized, they have a shape, they work as a team. They aren't animals. We just can't see what they are doing, what world they are living in, what they are thinking."

"What world are they living in?" said Smacksburg. "It's the same world as ours. Cut 'em with a knife, they'll bleed, shoot 'em in the head, they'll die. What world they are living in? Same as us and the wild pigs and the dogs and the wolves."

Smacksburg looked angry and Miranda was reminded of so many other angry men, drunks, strangers in bars, roommates, co-workers, yelling, pointing fingers, demanding to be taken seriously.

"Take it easy, Dave," Miranda said and he winked at her.

She had never felt so bored. So exhausted by conversation. It wasn't really the liquor and the drugs. Their performance sucked all the energy out of her, drained her. She could barely keep her eyes open. It took a force of will to take a drink now and then. She made herself pick up a stick and push white-hot embers around. She thought about that apartment she found on this side of the Appalachians, in the town with the feral dogs. She thought about dragging Arthur through the snowy streets. About the chickens. Puzzles. The darkness in the IKEA. She smiled to herself at what counted for nostalgia in her new circumstances. Smacksburg jumped to his feet.

"You're not fucking listening," he said. "They are fucking animals, dumb animals, not dolphins or dogs or monkeys, dumber than that, they are programmed or something, it's all instinct, all reaction, no thinking. Fucking vegetables."

"But they drive trucks from point A to point B," said Dave. "They ship food and gas. Animals can't do that kind of shit. Animals don't do logistics. Plants don't do logistics. Vegetables don't do logistics."

"Ants do," said Smacksburg.

Dave stared at him thoughtfully.

"It's radio waves," growled the skinny man and everyone turned to look at him.

"What's that, Fubar?" asked Smacksburg.

"It's radio waves," said Fubar. "They use those big radio telescopes NASA was using to look for aliens to get their orders from outer space. The ones out in the desert. Then they bounce the orders off satellites and into everyone's heads."

"Not my head," said Smacksburg. "Not my head. I don't hear no orders from outer space."

"Your head is broken," said Fubar. "And mine. And hers." He nodded at Miranda. Then at Dave: "And his."

Dave laughed, "Bent antenna."

Smacksburg frowned, took a swallow of vodka, and muttered something under his breath.

"That's right, Fubar," Dave tapped his head. "Substandard equipment, poor reception, corrupt signal."

"OK, guys." Miranda stood up unsteadily. "I'm going to bed."

She crawled into a sleeping bag in the back of a van and fell asleep to their raucous laughter. Dave was telling them about how he acquired his huge sack of weed. He met this scientist in New Jersey, he told them, who had worked for Monsanto, and now she had corporate greenhouse after corporate greenhouse filled with the plants.

"They were as big as palm trees!" Dave told them.

She woke to silence and darkness. Dave was not in the van. She crawled to the front and peered out. The fire had subsided to embers and Fubar was sitting by himself in the dull glow, head bowed. There was a light on in the caravan by the lake, the sky a flat black sheet behind it. She checked the glove compartment for the .45 and put it in a pocket of the door panel where she could reach it easily, then she pulled the sleeping bag up after her and curled up under it on the passenger seat. The next time she awoke the sky was a chill bone color and Dave was climbing into the driver's seat.

"Hey, what's up?" she asked.

"We're getting out of here," he said and started the motor. The engine coughed to life.

"What? Why?"

Dave was already turning the van around. Miranda looked out the window. Fubar was standing beside the ashes of the fire, a blanket pulled around his shoulders, black beard hanging in ropes from his chin, eyes glistening above cavernous cheeks, furrows gouged out of his forehead by his frown. Beyond him the meadow fell away, down into the hard, glittering lake and the washed-out liquid light of the rising sun.

"What's going on?"

"I didn't much like those guys," said Dave. He stank of alcohol and wood smoke and weed. "Didn't much care for them."

"No? They seemed to like you. Or at least your jokes."

"Anyone would. Fine jokes. Funny jokes. And I'm a likable guy. But that's got nothing much to do with my feelings about them, does it?"

"Did you get your stories? For your notebooks?"

"Oh yeah," he said and the van jerked and jumped over the ruts. "Yeah, I got my stories. These guys are no good. No good. We gotta leave."

"What happened?"

"Nothing happened."

"Something must have. You were all playing so nice around the fire. They even took you down to their caravan. Something happen down there?"

"Nothing happened," said Dave and twitched, the skin on his face shivered like something was crawling around under it. "Just stories exchanged. Words circulated. Redistributed. We have to go."

When they got to the gate Miranda opened it. Then they switched places and she drove them back down the lane and through the ruins of the restaurants and the gas stations and back out onto the highway. The sun was rising behind them and it looked like a beautiful day, but her mouth tasted terrible, she had a splitting headache, and her back hurt. Dave found some Percocet in the glove compartment, and she washed it down with a mouthful of lukewarm water from a plastic bottle.

"Where's the .45?" he asked.

"Door," she said and he fished it out and put it away.

It took a while before she settled into the rhythm of the road. The signs were all promising Cleveland. A couple of tankers came cruising out of the west and rattled past them, windshields lit up by the blank sun.

"Still working," muttered Dave. "Always working. Circulating. Circulating. Redistributing."

Dave was talking about Fubar's radio wave theory: "An oldie but a goodie. One of my favorites. A little minimalist, this version, a little stark, a little reduced. The most developed version I heard was out near Virginia Beach. An ex-navy guy who was sure he had it all figured out. He was even convinced he knew the frequency. I called him Kenneth but he refused to get the joke. He refused to get jokes in general. He was living under one of those old radio towers, in a little box under the antennae, in a room full of electronic equipment. It was like a massive needle jammed up under the skin of the sky. A hypodermic. He was broadcasting countersignals or some such madness, a single relentless note, trying to reverse the effect of the frequency or at least mute it. He called it his vaccination program. He was pumping code into the sky. The crazy bastard had done all kinds of complex calculations, was convinced he created a safe zone for miles around, was always looking for volunteers to help, to camp out at other antennae, other radio towers, to get the code circulating, to distribute it, to redistribute it, he had this vision of interlocking vaccinated zones, he was going to save the world with a dial tone."

His laughter dissolved into a ragged cough.

"You didn't sign up for his program?" asked Miranda.

"He had a stroke before I could."

"So what did you end up giving those guys for the gas?" Miranda asked.

"A lid of the weed, the OxyContin, that heroin from the truck stop. They'll be partying for a week or two, those guys. And we got enough fuel to make it to Chicago without stopping unless we want to."

"Well, that's good. So it wasn't all bad then. And the BBQ was sure tasty."

"Too much vinegar in the sauce," he said and then dug up one of his notebooks and started scribbling in it. It took fifteen minutes before the pen rolled onto the floor and he gently sagged forward against the seatbelt, head down, snoring.

At about noon they came across a destroyed tanker truck. Miranda slowed down and a fist of crows heaved themselves up off the ground and flapped heavily up to the power lines. Dave had rolled down the windows in the hopes the wind would help wake him up from his doziness and the van filled with the dizzying efflorescence of gas and the reek of burned tires. The blackened cab was on its side in a gore of melted rubber and glass, bent rimmed windows entirely vacant, the twisted wreckage of its scorched twin tanks trailing along the ditch behind it like guts still attached to the head of a fish. Miranda was starting to speed up again when they saw the first body, right where the crows had been. The figure lay on his side facing the fields, the back of its head a bloody mess, jeans soiled and legs askew, empty shell casings at his feet flashing in the sun, one arm pinned beneath, the other thrown back across the road. The second body was a dozen yards further down the highway, half in the ditch and half out, long legs stretched out in a thin V, one work boot almost on its side, the other pointed up like the gnomon on a sundial, casting its short shadow on the tarmac. The body lay across the verge, in the reeds and the grass, arms and head invisible. Miranda accelerated until they were cruising down the highway again at a comfortable speed, but it took some time for the wind to clean away the chemical stink, and the stink of shit and rotting meat and fear and shame.

6

THERE WAS A HAZE TO THE NORTH where Cleveland was supposed to be, a dark, drifting stain.

"What do you think?" Miranda asked.

"What do you think?" she asked again when he didn't answer. "Smoke? Fire? Is Cleveland burning?"

"I think we should keep heading west to Toledo and forget about Cleveland."

So they did, and Dave told Miranda about a dream he kept having, in which he returned to college to become an archeologist, and his professor, a woman of about his own age, had taken him and his fellow students to Mexico City for a dig.

"We were there for the Aztecs," said Dave. "You know how they are always finding new pyramids and temples under the roads and the sewers whenever there is construction? Well, in my dream there was an earthquake and a major road was split apart, one-half of the earth had risen above the other. You could walk along this brand new cliff that had appeared in the middle of the city, looking at the levels, at the sedimentation, at the four hundred years that passed since the conquistadores arrived, looking at the beautiful colors, the striations: tawny, amber, gold. And of course, there were the skeletal remains embedded in there too, and in my dream they were the remains of children, their little midget bones, their otherworldly bones."

He paused to gather his thoughts.

"We started digging there. To get deeper. Past those murdering bastards who came from Spain in 1492. Past the West. That was the project. Beneath those layers of what we were used to, the natural layers, somehow organic, layers that despite all the pottery shards and tin cans and detritus of modern life seemed somehow natural to us, those top layers, the ones closest to us, beneath them, beneath these natural but not natural layers we eventually got to the pre-Columbian years we were looking for and were confronted with the full weight of a different civilization, a different culture, there were actual walls now, evidence of massive structures, of buildings, you know, of work forces and organization and logistics, huge slabs of yellow and ochre stone carefully fitted, amazing carvings, blocks of intricate hieroglyphs, gods and heroes, lists of kings, chronicles of battles. Because they were murdering bastards too, weren't they? It's not just the West, never has been just the West. There've been so many killers, rapists, slavers, haven't there? So many. But anyways, neither here nor there. We kept digging down, me and the professor and the college kids, down, down, down, we descended deeper, building scaffolding as we went, climbing up and down, working under floodlights in the night, down, down, down, darker, colder, deeper. Eventually we got so deep the sunlight couldn't reach us and the lights were on all the time, cold white radiation, and the carvings began to change, as if under the influence of those lights as much as the passage of time, almost as if that was what it was, as if the light was making everything come apart, but of course it wasn't the light, it was time. The images began to sort of disintegrate, come apart, like I said, eyes drifting out of skulls, jaws detaching, feathered snakes unwinding into clouds of worms, a sort of disaggregation. I don't know what to call it. The symbols devolved until they were nothing but random, curving, curling gouges that went on and on, down, down, as deep as we could dig, thousands and thousands of years, hundreds of thousands, maybe even millions."

They stopped at a major interchange where the turnpike humped up over another highway. Right at the peak they got out and looked about, enjoyed the sun and wind in their hair. The world spread out around them in its endless circle of bush and haze and sky. Dave spread out his arms, closed his eyes, and let the air wash over him.

"Feel better?" Miranda asked when his arms dropped.

"I do," he said. "Let me drive a bit."

"I don't want to end up in a ditch. Or collide with a semi."

"Come on. I feel good. I'm in good shape. I can tell when the seizures are coming and they aren't."

They were driving through a region where there was once real industry, not the desperate start-ups and family operations of the Appalachians, not businesses kept alive on scraps of scrounged capital and government handouts, but huge factories, chemical and automobile plants, massive malls. Cleveland's greasy pall hung over it all and they could feel the smoke in their noses and lungs.

"Once those cities start burning," said Dave, "it takes a long time for them to run out of fuel. Miami burned for months. It was so bizarre because it was flooded at the same time, you know, at the same time as it burned. There were these people down there who would paddle down the saltwater streets, the submerged highways, between the sheets of towering flames, looking for canned goods and clothes and liquor, looking for drugs and guns and explosives, right there, right in the inferno. I went in with one of those guys, a swamp cracker who had it all going on, with the ragged beard and the MAGA ball cap and the OxyContin habit, but a good guy, still, a pretty good guy,

I liked him. We wore masks, you know, as we paddled about, firefighter gas masks with the tanks strapped to our bare backs, because of the smoke and the toxic clouds. You could feel the air rushing past, sucked into the city from the countryside to feed those fires, unholy winds transformed into jets of blazing light and thick, coiling columns of oily black smoke that blotted out the sky. Permanent twilight. We were on a sort of a punt that this guy poled about and there was life there, you know, especially the outskirts, there was quite a bit of life on the outskirts. This fellow told me he had once seen dolphins on a main thoroughfare, racing through the water against a backdrop of orange flames, and I saw a stingray undulating underneath us, passing over a manhole cover. In the suburbs it was all greasy soap water and scum and stinking of rotten eggs and gas. There were manatees and alligators there, plenty of them. But as you got downtown, towards the central business district I guess you'd call it, the fires got too hot for anything but humans, and rats, they were there, swimming about, hunched up on window sills and the tops of traffic lights, and cockroaches, plenty of them, but too hot for anything natural, anything wild, only feral creatures stayed. It was too dangerous for anything that wasn't unnaturally greedy, unnaturally curious: explosions and firestorms whipped up by the rotating winds. The whole harbor was on fire, a lake of burning oil. You could see the charred corpses of the cruise ships. You could watch the fiery twisters dancing across the open spaces."

Dave was back in the passenger seat after lunch. Miranda ate cold beans from the can on the side of the road, watching the vultures cycling through the updrafts. Dave wandered off into a gas station looking for a toilet and was gone a long time.

He came back with a few tubes of Pringles and a six-pack of Diet Coke in cans.

"It actually flushed," he had said. "There was water in the tank, can you believe it?"

He ate a couple of Pringles and tilted the tube at Miranda. She shook her head.

"What a fantastic sound it was," Dave had said, "the most beautiful sound in the world, clean and refreshing, divine, a divine sound, the sound of angels singing."

He tossed Miranda a can.

"Diet?" she asked.

"Sorry," Dave laughed. "Wasn't concentrating, all I could think about was that flushing sound."

"The sweeteners go bad," Miranda tossed the can back to him. "It'll be flat and taste terrible."

"I don't care," Dave said and cracked the can. "I want a Coke."

They left the cans lying scattered about the parking lot where Dave had thrown them one by one, in a fit of frustration and rage at their awful taste. But he was still working his way through the Pringles as they drove.

"Apparently there are some folks in Toledo," he said, "who have things set up pretty nice."

"Oh?"

"That little one told me about it, the asshole," said Dave. "Smacksburg. After you went to bed and the party moved to the caravan."

Miranda waited.

"Said these people in Toledo organized themselves into some kind of a community. He didn't seem very impressed. Said they were soft. Queer. But he said they were there. He scouted Toledo after he left Cleveland. Sussed them out. Spied on them. Not that long ago, he said. Watched them from across the river. Said they would still be there, for sure, they weren't going anywhere."

"Scouted?" asked Miranda.

"His word," said Dave. "The little Nazi turd. Not mine. Not my word."

III

THE TOWER

1

A NATTILY DRESSED MIDDLE-AGED MAN called Adrian took them up to the top of a very tall tower overlooking the Maumee River in Toledo. There were rain barrels and solar panels scattered about the flat roof, but the people in the building hadn't figured out how to connect them to the plumbing and electricity. They hauled them up in the early days, when they were still struggling to make sense of what happened and would happen, and it seemed like a good idea at the time, but once they reached the summit no one had known how to proceed, so the equipment sat there. Dave and Miranda found them, the Toledo Citizens Co-operative, when they spotted the impotent panels' shine, a bright blister of light on the building roof. They picked their way through the deserted streets and over an empty bridge until they reached the tower, a shard of steel, stone, and glass rising out of the cracked concrete and crumbling tar, a few people working in the vegetable gardens at its base.

This man, Adrian, excited they had noticed the panels, immediately marched them up what seemed endless flights of dark staircases, illuminating the dust and cobwebs and the rat droppings with paraffin lamps. They stopped about three times before, sweating and out of breath, they pushed open a creaking door and stepped into the pristine air.

"There used to be almost a hundred people here," Adrian told them. "When we started lugging this stuff up here. It was quite an operation."

He was very proud of it. The operation. The Toledo Citizens Co-operative. The view from the tower.

And delighted to have them.

He kept telling them.

He would push his glasses up his nose.

"Delighted to have you," he would say. "Delighted. As guests. So pleased to be able to show you around. So proud, really, proud of what we have accomplished, of what we will."

Dave would enthusiastically encourage him.

"But of course there are fewer of us now than when we started." Adrian was wearing neatly pressed khaki trousers, a white-and-blue checked shirt, leather shoes, and glasses with a gunmetal frame. "Heart attacks and strokes and so on. So, there are a few empty apartments. A few free spaces."

He worked hard to include them both in his conversation but Miranda was uninterested. She wandered over to the north side of the tower and the two men followed her.

"We have plenty of food, not only the scavenged cans so many people are dependent on, but the fresh vegetables we grow here. And we staked out some greenhouses on the other side of the river. That means fresh vegetables in the winter as well. Eventually, we will reclaim some old fields for soybeans and corn and potatoes. Not that there aren't plenty of potential calories available in the downtown area – pigs and dogs, of course, but also frogs, insects, birds, rodents and other small mammals. We had a nutritionist who did a study. Not appealing, bugs and pests, but we have to adapt to circumstances. And really, even in the tower itself we have enough stored to maintain our current population in relative comfort almost indefinitely. In a pinch we could close shop and not have to venture out for years."

"Why would you have to do that?" asked Dave.

"I couldn't possibly imagine," said Adrian. "But these are strange times."

"Zombies?" asked Dave. "Roving bands of cannibals? A plague? Starving wolves?"

"Well," said Adrian and laughed weakly. "At least not the zombies. It turns out they're harmless."

They ignored his joke.

The brown river emptied out into Lake Erie a few miles upstream. Most of the downtown and suburbs were reclaimed by untamed bush but the main arteries were kept clear: the big east-west roads and those heading south. And, on the side of the river they had just come from, a harbor and a stretch of industrial land could be seen from their vantage point. A couple of tankers were docked by hazy jetties, and a long braid of train track and interlocking pipes connected them and the lake to a sprawling, steaming refinery; to long dusty lots of coal, of iron; to lots full of parked semis; to all the various infrastructure of the old productivity.

"The diggers have the refinery working," said Dave.

"They do," Adrian cleared his throat and pushed his glasses up his nose. "I personally think they have it close to its previous capacity, I used to count the trucks and in one twenty-four hour period last August a little over 500 trucks rolled out of there. At 200 barrels a truck, that's at least 100,000 barrels. It was their busiest day ever, but still, they do keep plugging away."

"Crazy," said Dave. "That's so crazy. How the hell do they do it?"

Adrian shrugged.

"Radio waves," said Miranda. It was the first thing she said since their arrival.

Dave snorted and Adrian pushed his glasses up his nose.

Adrian's apartment was five floors above the street and had Persian rugs, marble countertops and floor-to-ceiling windows that gave him a view of the lake. A woman of about forty in a dark blue dress sat in a chair staring out at the haze and water. Her greying hair was put up to show her earrings and she had gold around her neck, at her wrists, and on her fingers. She did not look at them when they entered.

"That's my wife, Ella," Adrian said and ushered them over to the island in the kitchen.

"A drink?" he asked. "Wine? Beer? Cocktail?"

"Some water, please," said Miranda, but Dave was excited about the wine. Adrian gave her a glass of cool, limpid water and began to show Dave his many bottles. Dave became extra effusive, so Miranda went to the windows to watch the clouds forming over Lake Erie. She stood a few feet away from Ella but the woman did not acknowledge her, just kept staring at the slowly changing blues and whites and greys of sky. Miranda caught the occasional word from the kitchen but barely registered them: "chateau something something something," "an auspicious vintage," "a blend of blah blah blah."

One of the tankers was leaving the distant docks, sliding out into the quartz glitter of the lake. Seagulls drifted through the air between her and the water. Far to the east, she could see the discoloration on the horizon that was Cleveland.

They ate a light supper on the marble island: arugula with a mellow vinaigrette; fat slices of tomato; shards of actual, slightly funky, parmesan; cold chicken; a dark, heavy loaf of bread. Dave and Adrian were so excited about the chardonnay they opened that she agreed to have a glass. Ella did not join them.

After they ate, Adrian took them out to meet the neighbors. Across the dark, carpeted hall was Gerald Monroe, who was fifty and wore a silk shirt and a watch, next to him Sarah and Sam Waterman, who, like Adrian and Ella, were married after "The Event," and like them, dressed immaculately. On the next floor down were Mel and Greg, who had a two-year-old and an infant. They were the youngest children Miranda had seen since she left the East Coast. Their white skin looked unimaginably soft. She could smell soap and baby powder and a bright citrus cleaner. The children's fingers were fat sausages and both had shining blue eyes and downy blond hair. She couldn't stop staring at them. She wanted to touch them – no, wanted wasn't the word. She was starving for a touch of their delicate skin, ravenous, she wanted to pinch them, kiss them, eat them. She was at the same time intensely aware of her dirtiness, her filthy jeans and stained jacket, the greasy hair lank in her eyes, the stink of her pits, her crotch, her feet, the stink coming off Dave too, and his now ragged-looking hair, his exhausted face, the stains on his trousers and the elbows on his leather jacket rubbed raw and bare. Mel's gaze fluttered between whoever was talking and Miranda staring at the kids.

On that floor were also a few doors on which Adrian did not knock.

The apartments were all so tidy, so absurdly hygienic, and everyone was so well-dressed, everything was so well put together that Miranda's throat tightened as soon as they walked into a room. She began to have flashbacks to scattered moments of childhood shame, to wet sheets and bathroom accidents and the wrong clothes for the wrong event and all manner of half-forgotten catastrophes. In the stairwell to the next floor Adrian finally commented that Miranda's energy was flagging and suggested they pack it in for the night, and meet the rest of the Co-op members in the morning.

He led them into a two-bedroom apartment facing the setting sun, which he called the guest suite. He showed them the canned goods in the pantry, the neatly appointed bedrooms, the bathroom with the soft towels and its stacked jugs of water.

"Feel free to use as much as you want," he said. "You needn't ration yourself. But please refill them from the barrels on the roof before you go."

In the living room there were boxes of candles, lamps and a TV with a small DVD library.

"One day soon, we will have the electricity to make use of those," he said, waving at the discs. "If you arrived a year or two from now, I'm sure we would have had the power hooked up, you would have been able to watch whatever you liked."

Then he said goodnight and left.

Dave went straight to the DVD collection and began to flip

through it.

"Was it my imagination," he said. "Or did all those folks loot exactly the same department stores?"

It was getting dark and Miranda lit the lamp.

"Holy shit," said Dave and pulled out a DVD. "The Warriors. How is this even possible?"

He lowered his voice to a rumble: "That...is a miracle. And miracles is the way things ought to be."

"You seen this?" he asked. "You seen this? If you haven't I can recite the whole goddam thing for you."

"You're on your own," Miranda said. "I'm getting clean."

She took a few candles and went to the bathroom. After she arranged them on the vanity and lit them, she stripped down and stared at herself in the mirror. In the flickering light she looked orange and grotesque. She stared at her long limbs and her ribs, and the absurd cloud of pubic hair. She thought of those children again. And of Mel, of how the mother's skin looked almost as pale and soft as that of the children, her hair as blonde, eyes as blue. She thought of Mel's full breasts pushing against the fabric of her blouse. She poured a few jugs of water into the tub, thinking of all those stairs to the roof. She could hear Dave reciting lines from his movie in the living room and detect the bright tang of his weed behind the waxy floral scent of the candles.

"Everybody says Cyrus is the one and only," she heard Dave say. "And I gave him my word we would uphold the truce."

There were only a couple of inches of tepid water to slide into but there was a smooth, beautifully rounded, entirely unused bar of white soap waiting for her. She picked it up, weighed it in her hand, felt its heft, so dense and smooth she wanted to take a bite out of it. She would steal it, she decided, as she worked it up into a lather. She would take it. Dave could find his own soap. There must be more bars under the sink. He could have one of those, but this one was hers. And when they left this place she would take it with her. She would steal it. She would steal it. It was hers.

2

IN THE MORNING THE TOUR THROUGH the shadowy halls continued: more immaculate couples and elegant individuals, oblique conversations about circumstances and situations and best solutions, and many closed doors, many more. Behind some of these closed doors, Adrian suggested, were more Co-op members, and behind others, nothing.

They met a former architect with a Le Corbusier chaise longue on the fifth floor who said, "I feel like what the Co-op offers is not simply comfort and a modicum of convenience, but hope. By maintaining peaceable order in the chaos, we are also curating important civilizational values. Did you know we are establishing a library on the middle floors in which we will gather as many literary artifacts as we can from our immediate urban and suburban environs? And eventually, maybe, from the whole region."

A former lawyer with the three aging, brittle lapdogs he called Yorkies lived on the fourth: "I like the thought that we are all participating in something greater than our own immediate survival, that this improvised egalitarian world we are struggling so hard to maintain is, in a small way, preparation for a future in which the achievements of the old world which is gone will be recognized by new generations, learned from, and surpassed."

The former music teacher with the baby grand and the former sociologist with the art collection shared a creative space on the third: "We finally feel safe." "When we moved in here we were so tired." "Exhausted, really." "From the grind of just staying alive." "Now we have time for reading and music and art." "For real work!" "For hope, really!"

Everyone elected to live on the south side of the building and their carefully arranged tableaux were flooded with sunlight, cheerful and perfect, but the hallways between them were dark and gloomy. To Miranda it started to feel like they had wandered offstage when they were in the halls, behind the scenes, auditioning people for parts in a play about the banality of modern life. Or in a museum or an aquarium, walking from display to display, from performance to performance, and she began to feel a burnt-out, overwhelmed feeling from the long stretch of overstimulation. She was tired of listening to Adrian and Dave repeat the same words of introduction over and over, tired of feigning interest in people she could not distinguish from each other without the help of empty professional and social designations. She was tired of people. They had been there less than twelve hours.

"I'm going to step outside," Miranda said after they closed the door on the music teacher and the sociologist, and Adrian's eyebrows shot up.

"Oh," he said and pushed his glasses up his nose. "I see."

Dave was grinning at Miranda over Adrian's shoulder.

"There's only a few more people on this floor," said Adrian. "Then we're done."

"You and Dave go ahead," said Miranda. "I'm going outside."

"Uh, yeah," said Dave. "I think I could do with some fresh air myself."

"I see," said Adrian.

Outside the building, a modest cluster of skyscrapers provided a bulwark against the elements; cool indirect sunlight drifted down to ground level between the shafts of the buildings and illuminated a maze of box gardens. A breeze coiled in and out of the buildings, slipping across pedestrian malls and empty streets, making pansies and daffodils quiver and tremble. Young tomatoes and sweet peas shivered against their stakes. An old man in a denim jacket and toque pulled weeds methodically from the flowerbeds.

Adrian led Dave and Miranda to a picnic table and produced a thermos of coffee, paper cups, and some muffins from his satchel.

They ate in silence, watching the old man work.

"His name is Eli Bird," Adrian finally said. "He used to be a sculptor. Quite famous, you could even say celebrated."

"You sure have a lot of creative types living in this building," said Dave. "Very upscale bohemian, very Soho, very Architectural Digest, a very gentrified sort of post-apocalypse you all have organized."

Adrian smiled, a little tightly.

"Eli doesn't actually live with us anymore," he said. "He moved down by the river, to the yacht club, but we make sure he has enough to eat and we let him keep his beds in the communal gardens."

"You let him?" Dave grinned. "A little patch of private property in your socialist paradise."

Adrian launched into a long exposition about creativity and mental health and mixed-market socialism, which Dave kept interrupting with little witticisms. The roads around the building were in impeccable condition. There were no weeds growing on them, and it looked to Miranda like someone made an attempt to patch the potholes with a thin tar. The storefronts, too, were well-kept, the few broken windows neatly boarded over. Down the side roads she caught glimpses of a more general decline: weeds, scrubby plants, rusting fire escapes, cracks in the façade.

The conversation beside her became a little heated. No one's voices were raised, but the temperature had definitely increased since she stopped paying attention. Adrian stood up and said something about decorum loudly and sharply, then walked over to Eli.

"I think you might have pissed him off," said Miranda.

"He pissed me off," said Dave. "Always talking to us like we're trying to join his country club."

When Adrian came back he brought Eli over to meet them.

"Eli, this is Dave and this is Miranda. They arrived yesterday from out east."

He was a small, dark, slightly bent man with a ragged white beard, heavy brows, and almost-black eyes. He quivered, and tremors shook his body. Dave stood up and offered his hand. Miranda nodded.

"Out east? Through Cleveland?" Eli asked.

"Not Cleveland," said Adrian.

"No," said Dave. "Didn't swing by. Had a bad feeling about visiting Cleveland. Didn't we, Miranda?"

"We did," said Miranda.

"Your feeling wasn't wrong," said Eli and coughed.

He sat down at the picnic table. So did Dave and Adrian.

"Bad times in Cleveland," said Eli. "Bad times all around. Extra bad in Cleveland."

He pulled out a ziplock bag of tobacco and some papers, hands shaking. He started rolling but kept spilling little coils of the stuff, little strings. He let nothing go to waste, pinching each stray strand between trembling fingers and returning it to its paper cradle. They all watched as he struggled.

"You grow that?" Dave asked.

"I do," said Eli. "But not here. Down by the river. I moved into the old Marina. The Co-op doesn't approve of smoking."

"Eli, please," said Adrian. "Be nice, be neighborly."

"You want one?" Eli offered his rumpled little cigarette to Dave.

"Sure," said Dave and took it. He fished a lighter out of his pocket and Eli began to roll another one. Dave blew a few plumes of smoke up and away from Adrian. He sighed from the pleasure of it.

When Eli finally had his cigarette ready he wasn't as polite as Dave. He lit up and gassed them with clouds of sweet white smoke. Adrian tried not to give him the satisfaction of coughing.

"We're having a little soirée tonight, Eli," said Adrian. "In honor of our guests. We get so few. Why don't you throw on something nice and pop by?"

"No thanks," said Eli.

"Why not? You used to love a party back in the old days. You used to be at all the events. You loved culture."

"What's culture?" said Eli. "I can't remember."

Adrian laughed brightly, then frowned and adjusted his glasses: "It's what makes us human. It's what separates us from the animals. Deliberate behavior that has no obvious utilitarian purpose but to give pleasure."

Eli raised an eyebrow.

"Pleasure," said Adrian. "Culture is pleasure. It's a party. Come to the party. We miss you."

A man and woman who appeared to be in their fifties came out of the building and began puttering with the tomato plants.

"I'll be right back," said Adrian and hopped up. "I need to have a word with Franz and Lois."

"Late with their condo fees?" asked Eli and Adrian couldn't stop the eye roll.

"Back in a sec," he said to Miranda and darted off.

"God," said Dave, looking up at the buildings towering over them. "I hate skyscrapers."

"Oh yeah." said Eli.

"Makes me think of gravestones. And gravestones make me think of death."

"What's death make you think of?" asked Eli.

"My kids," said Dave. "Death makes me think of my kids."

Eli grunted.

"I hate them too," said Eli after a while.

"Skyscrapers?" asked Dave.

"Yup," said Eli.

"You got dead kids as well?"

"Yes, but that's not why I hate skyscrapers," said Eli. "I hate skyscrapers because they get in the way of my view."

After he finished his cigarette, Eli said his goodbyes and wandered off. Adrian brought Franz and Lois over. They were a small couple, shy as hedgehogs, tremulous and kind. Franz wore a baggy cardigan and had bad posture, a bald dome, and watery eyes behind thick glasses. Lois had short-cropped hair, an Ohio State sweatshirt, a long printed skirt, and sandals over thick grey socks.

They talked with Miranda about all the plants, about the benefits and drawbacks of what they called square-foot gardening, about growing seasons, about things that bored Dave so much he kept interrupting to keep himself entertained.

A few more people drifted out of the tower to enjoy the sunshine and the plants. Adrian introduced them all to Dave and Miranda.

Once new people stopped appearing, Dave produced his weed and started rolling a joint. Adrian frowned.

"Really?" Dave laughed. "You serious?"

"Well," said Adrian. "We don't care for drugs, no. We try to keep things balanced and healthy here. What one does in private, of course, is, well, private, but we are worried about, well, we want a functional society and that means, well, we agreed: no drugs."

"Just the Chardonnay then?" said Dave. "Maybe a bottle of Sangiovese now and then?"

Adrian's mouth tightened.

"Sorry," said Dave, and he actually reached out and touched Adrian's hand. "I clearly keep irritating you, huh? Am I being a dick? Not used to social nicety. Not used to civilized company. Not really. I've been on my own for so long, I'm not used to people. If I said the weed was medicinal, would that make it alright? For my seizures? Because it is. As well as the getting high. I do like that about it. But the stuff also helps keep me upright."

Adrian relaxed into a smile.

"Of course," he said. "I know we seem so prudish and square but it's how we get along. With our silly rules. Maybe just don't advertise it too much, for the time being, be a little discreet."

"No problem," said Dave and he stood up. "I'll pretend it's high school and go smoke my weed behind the gym."

Adrian and Miranda watched him wander off, a stooped figure

strolling through the gardens, stopping to chat with the people he passed, until finally he was out on the empty street, and then he dwindled away into the shadows between the buildings.

"You haven't had much to say, Miranda," Adrian said. "About any of this. About the Co-op."

"No," said Miranda. "I suppose I haven't."

"I am curious to know what you are thinking."

"So am I," said Miranda and Adrian cocked his head.

"I think slowly," said Miranda. "That's all. And not out loud. I haven't reached any conclusions yet."

"Not like Dave, then," said Adrian.

"Don't let his chatter fool you," Miranda said. "That's a cover. All those words are the dust he kicks up for cover so he can evaluate you."

"Really?"

Miranda looked away. She felt his bright eyes on her, crawling on her like spiders, felt him leaning in, trying to get her attention.

"How did you two meet?"

"I crashed my bike north of Pittsburgh and he showed up out of the blue and offered me a lift."

"A lift to where?"

"He was going out west to see the sights. And he daydreams about finding someone to make fresh pharmaceuticals. I used to have people up in Minnesota I'm looking for."

"I see," said Adrian. "So you'll both be moving on?"

"That's the plan," said Miranda.

"Do you have much hope your people will be up there now? In Minnesota?"

"No," said Miranda. "I have no hope at all. Neither does Dave."

They sat in silence for quite some time but Adrian kept crossing and re-crossing his legs, leaning forward and leaning back. The sun was starting to heat the air, beginning to inspire small atmospheric movements in the spaces between the buildings. A very mild breeze was drifting through. Miranda closed her eyes, felt the light falling across her lids, heard the chirp-chirp-chirp of a goldfinch, then realized there were some bees buzzing about. She was suddenly sitting on the deck at the lake with Dad, the same buzzing of the insects, the same warm summer air sliding like oil over her skin, the sunlight shattering on the diamond waves of the lake. He had just cracked his first beer of the day. It was a startlingly concrete memory but Miranda had no idea of the event that produced it, the period in which it was manufactured. It could have been from high school. Or college. It could be from the last summer before the digging started. There were no clues specific enough to fix it in place: simply her and Dad on the deck, the breeze blowing in off the water, washing through the poplars, neither of them saying a word.

"As I said to Eli, we're having a little party this evening." Adrian said. "To celebrate your visit. We get so few people coming through whose company we can truly enjoy."

3

ADRIAN CAME DOWN TO COLLECT Miranda and Dave in the early evening when there was enough light in the apartment that they hadn't lit any candles or lamps yet. He brought a lavender shirt and a silk tie for Dave and a black cocktail dress for Miranda.

"You look about the same size as Ella," he said.

"I'm sure I do," Miranda said. "But I'm not putting that on."

Adrian's smile slipped just a titch.

"What about you, Dave?" he asked. "You in the mood to dress up?"

"Sure." Dave was already a little drunk. "Sure, Adrian. That's a fantastic tie. Fantastic."

"Silk isn't really the style, anymore," said Adrian. "Or it wasn't any longer when such things mattered, but I felt the color was perfect for you, and why not luxuriate in the texture? Why not luxuriate?"

"Indeed," said Dave. "Luxuriate. Why not?"

He seized the clothes and swept into the bathroom.

"Are you sure, Miranda?" Adrian laid out the black dress on the couch. "It's a beautiful dress. Alexander McQueen."

"It is beautiful," said Miranda.

"Come touch it." Adrian rubbed the fabric gently between his thumb and forefinger. He was bent over it, very precisely, his back and neck straight, the creases of his shirt and pants following the angles of his body perfectly. The cut of his salt-and-pepper hair was astonishingly neat, the fade on his neck sublimating into the skin. "It's crepe wool."

Miranda did. It felt lovely.

"I'll do your hair too," said Adrian. "It will be fun."

The former music teacher and the former sociologist were hosting the party at their apartment. Late evening light was drifting in through the windows but lit candles were arranged throughout the living room. The furniture was pushed to the sides and folding chairs were set up in a half circle around the baby grand – itself covered with candles. A cello, a chair and a music stand stood beside it now. Two dozen people in fine clothes milled about, sipping wine and cocktails. There were plates of fresh vegetables, smoked fish, and crudités Adrian had prepared. Dave was talking to a few people whose names Miranda could not remember. She could not remember their former occupations either; they were shapes, empty forms.

Dave was gesturing towards the east, towards the direction they came from, and Miranda could catch the occasional word or phrase but not much more. She thought it was a story she had already heard a few times, a long one about an epileptic helicopter pilot he knew, who flew up and down the East Coast photographing the digs, who used to take Dave up with him on his exploratory flights.

"They called him Roulette," was Dave's punchline. "When he was bored he used to frighten me by pretending to have seizures and the helicopter would fall earthwards. Funny guy."

Greg, from Greg and Mel, was in the kitchen by himself, nursing a Bud. Miranda went over to where he stood.

"Mel with the kids?" she asked.

"Yeah," said Greg. He was tall, heavy, maybe twenty-five or twenty-six, blond hair already receding, ruddy cheeks. "Hard to get a babysitter these days, you know? So only one of us can ever come to Adrian's soirées."

"You drew the short straw."

"Naaah, I don't mind these things. I like to see who's still out and about, who doesn't show up anymore. But Mel hates them. She didn't mind them in the early years, but since the kids –" he shrugged and took a swig.

"Surely that's not an actual Bud?"

"Nope. Homemade. But as near a facsimile of a clear, bland lager as I can manage. I put them in the labeled bottles to irritate Adrian. He thinks I'm a rube. A classless jerk."

"Are you?"

"Isn't everyone now? Classless?"

"I don't know about that," said Miranda. "Hard to say. Haven't seen enough people to make a judgement. Dave would be the guy to ask, he pays attention to that sort of thing."

"You look fabulous, by the way," said Greg.

"Do I?"

"Yes, you do," said Greg. "Where'd you get the dress?"

"Adrian. It's Ella's."

"Really?" his eyebrows shot up.

"Why is that such a surprise?"

"Because since her palsy kicked in the whole apartment has been an unchanging shrine to what Adrian thinks she used to be."

He waited for her to say something but she was looking out the windows and the smear of clouds across the horizon,

"A frigid bitch." He drained his bottle. "She used to be a frigid bitch."

Miranda glanced at him.

"Ella," he said. "A bit of a cunt, really. Don't much miss having her around. Want to try a fake Bud?"

"I'll stick with the real Chardonnay, thanks," said Miranda and turned away as he went to the fridge.

Dave was still holding forth, his audience even larger. Adrian drifted over to hover at her arm.

"I wonder if Eli will make an appearance."

"I don't think so."

"Well, he might, mightn't he? Don't you think? He was a little noncommittal, to be sure, but still."

"I thought it was a pretty clear no."

Adrian frowned.

"He's such a strange man," he said. "Utterly indifferent to conversation."

"Some people are introverted."

"It's something else with him," said Adrian. "He's never been shy. It's a tactic. He's lost in some scheme, some plan that has nothing to do with us anymore, nothing to do with humanity. And it's deliberate. Provocative."

Miranda said nothing, so Adrian laughed too loudly: "I don't know. I'm being silly."

"That's a change." Greg was back.

"Oh hullo, Greg," said Adrian brightly. "Glad you could make it. No Mel tonight? Stuck at home with the squalling brood?"

"Adrian doesn't care for children," said Greg. "Doesn't see the point."

"Greg's half-right, as usual." Adrian pushed his glasses up his nose. "I do, actually, see the point."

Franz and Lois entered the apartment and looked about nervously.

Franz looked lost and tired in a rumpled suit. Lois wore a yellow sundress with a white shawl draped over her shoulders. She saw Miranda and smiled.

"Excuse me," said Miranda and went over to Lois to talk about gardening.

It was almost dark by the time Adrian seated all of them in

their gloomy rows and was clearing his throat.

"Good afternoon," he said and glanced out the windows at the rosy sky. "Or rather, good evening."

He insisted Dave and Miranda sit at the front. The former music teacher was at the piano. A tall woman sat at a cello. The cellist wore black dress pants and a severe white shirt that had mellowed into yellow and then orange as the light changed.

"Of course, any excuse for a soirée is welcome, but today really is special, and all of this," Adrian waved weakly about and cleared his throat again, "this is all to honor our guests Dave Boyd and Miranda, um, sorry Miranda, I don't know your last name."

"Miranda is fine," said Miranda.

Greg laughed in the back somewhere.

"Dave Boyd and Miranda, then, welcome," said Adrian. "Perhaps you'd each like to briefly introduce yourself to our little community? A few words about where you're from? What you do?"

Dave stood up and turned around.

"I'm Dave Boyd," he said. "I'm originally from Virginia Beach but that was a long time ago. I used to be a high school math teacher. Now I travel around, collect stories, ask people about their lives, how they live, how they make sense of things."

"Like an anthropologist," suggested Adrian.

"Sure," said Dave. "Maybe more of a folklorist though."

"Like the Brothers Grimm," suggested Adrian.

"Sure," said Dave. "Brothers Grimm. Or Studs Terkel. Something like that."

"Tell us a story," Greg shouted from the back.

"Sure," said Dave. Adrian pushed his glasses up his nose. "One of the most widely distributed stories I have come across is the Dog-Killing Goat Boy. So, there are many different versions of this. Sometimes even within the same region. Like in the Virginia Beach area, where I first started hearing it a few months after the change, there were at least five distinct accounts. In one township it was told consistently one way, in another it was told by the folks there with minor changes. Then when I hit the road, I found it everywhere up and down the East Coast, and in the larger towns on this side of the Appalachians. Usually an urban or a suburban story."

Adrian coughed.

"Right," said Dave and his hand twitched. "Y'all asked for a story, now you're going to have to sit tight and listen."

There was muted laughter. Miranda was watching the former music teacher. She was sitting at the piano; hands in lap – one clenched and the other open, facing upwards, the two shorter fingers curled inwards, the fore and index fingers loosely extended and thumb arched; shoulders slumped; head eerily cocked and thrust forward; staring blankly at the sheet music. There was something very fixed about her, constructed, and the depth of the shadows behind her reminded Miranda of baroque paintings. The word chiaroscuro leapt up in her mind.

"It's always a skinny kid. Usually of the storyteller's race; white folks talk about a white kid, black folks a black kid."

"In the story?" Adrian interrupted. "They mention his race in the story?"

"Not usually," said Dave. "But I always ask. I'm practically a professional, see? I'm analytical. I'm thinking all the time, asking the right questions, the important questions, the acute ones."

"Right," said Adrian. "Of course."

"So, it's a skinny kid with yellow eyes. Sometimes he has a skinny little tail or stubby horns, sometimes he has a hoof on one foot, sometimes he's naked with a huge red cock, bright red, sometimes he's in rags or rough hides, sometimes he's on foot, sometimes he rips around on a dirt bike. Sometimes he's local, lives in the woods or the holler or by the dump. Sometimes he travels from town to town. And he kills all the dogs. All the feral dogs. That's the big theme. That's the trope, I guess you could call it. Something like that. He's a scalawag, mostly. A trickster figure. You have to give him food if you see him, or if you think he's around, or there'll be trouble. Dead sheep in the well. All the chickens killed. That kind of thing. Leave him tobacco and liquor. Lots of people do this. Lots of folks. He tricks women into sleeping with him too, uses disguises, drugs them, creeping into the dark bedroom when the husband is out late, he impregnates them and they give birth to puppies. Yellow-eyed puppies. He rapes the digger women too: same result. Yellow-eyed puppies. But mostly he kills adult dogs. Shoots them, or sets traps, or poisons them and then hangs their bodies on trees. In some versions he skins them and wears their pelts. In some he eats them. And there are some deeply fucked-up versions of this story too. In my favorite one, from near Durham, NC, this old man down there claimed he found the Goat Boy's lair, a deserted tobacco warehouse under a water tower with an old Lucky Strikes logo painted on it. This old guy said the Goat Boy only killed the male dogs, kept all the bitches to himself and would copulate with them, although he didn't use the word copulate, he said Goat Boy fucked them, fucked them all the time, and when he wasn't fucking them he'd roll around and play with them, sleep in a big tangled mass of them, love them altogether, and whenever they gave birth to the little yellow-eyed puppies he would cut the throats of the males and throw them to the pack to be torn apart."

Dave looked pretty pleased with himself

"Thank you, Dave, for that fascinating piece of ethnography," said Adrian. "And what about you, Miranda? Why don't you tell us something about yourself? Where you're from? Where you went to college?"

"I think I'll pass, Adrian, thanks," said Miranda. "I don't much care to talk about the old days."

"Well," said Adrian. "Why would you, I suppose? It is a bit melancholic, after all, morbid even, I suppose, and besides, as Dave has just illustrated, we live in much more fascinating times than we used to, times in which the days are filled with, um, incident."

Dave sat down and crossed his long legs.

"Thank you again, Dave," Adrian nodded at him, "For the

marvelous example of folk creativity. Now Sheila and Catherine will provide us with another sort of entertainment. This evening they are going to play Franz Liszt's Liebestraum for us."

There was a smattering of applause. The former music teacher glanced around, straightened her back and waited for the cello to begin its moan.

A few minutes into the performance, Miranda was startled from her reverie by a commotion in the back of the room. She sensed a wave of disturbance moving through the audience. Everyone was twisting in their chairs, looking over their shoulders, synchronized, a school of fish, starlings, and Adrian was hissing: "Keep playing, keep playing, it's nothing."

Franz had fallen from his chair in the back row and was trying to get back up. Lois was kneeling beside him, hands fluttering like birds, eyes rolling. The people nearest to them were leaning away, toward the walls and each other.

"Keep playing," Adrian hissed.

Dave shot out of his chair and ran over to Franz, pushing past people. Mrs. Waterman almost fell out of her chair as he brushed past her, but her husband caught her arm.

Miranda followed Dave to the stricken man.

"Smile," Dave said. "Can you smile?"

Franz stared at him, corners of his mouth pulled down in a grimace, eyes wide. Lois dropped her shawl and one of the straps of her sundress slipped off.

The music continued.

Miranda knelt beside Lois and put the shawl back on her shoulders and an arm around her.

"Can you lift your arms, Franz? Can you lift your arms?" asked Dave.

The cello stopped but the piano continued. Franz blinked a couple of times and then his eyes rolled up into his head.

People were standing, staring at Franz. Behind them were the windows, and beyond that the world was a black void. Lois began to cry deep frightened childish sobs.

"Franz?" said Dave. "Franz?"

Miranda looked back to the front of room. The former music teacher had finally stopped, her hands folded on her lap, staring out at the confusion. The bow was hanging at the cellist's side. Adrian's face was pale, lips tightly drawn, eyes bugged out, brow furrowed.

Dave checked Franz's pulse, listened to his breathing.

"Help me roll him onto his side," said Dave and Miranda did.

Lois regained a measure of composure.

"Has he had a history of strokes?" Dave asked.

"No," said Lois weakly.

"How's his blood pressure?"

"Fine," she said. "I don't know."

People were drifting towards the door. The cellist was starting to pack up.

The former sociologist was standing next to them.

"I think he had a stroke," said Dave. "Is there a history of strokes in his family?"

"I don't know," said Lois. "I don't know very much about him. We don't know each other very well."

"Well, he can't stay here," said the former sociologist.

Dave looked thoughtfully at Franz.

"Adrian," said the former sociologist. "He can't stay here. You said everyone would be gone by ten. You said you would help tidy up."

The former music teacher was still blankly watching them.

"Yes, I know, I know." Adrian came over and looked at Dave.

"He can't stay here," said Adrian, "he absolutely must be moved."

"God, you're an officious little prick." Greg had come over as well.

"It's nothing to do with me," said Adrian. "It's not my apartment."

"Well," said Dave. "Let's carry him home then."

Lois began to cry again.

"What a disappointment," said Adrian. "What a mess."

Miranda borrowed a sheet from the former sociologist and Adrian was sent to collect some broom handles and duct tape for a makeshift stretcher. Once made, Greg and Dave carried Franz through the unlit halls to the rooms he shared with Lois and laid him on a tidy bed. Then they left Miranda sitting in the living room with Lois.

"I don't know what to do," Lois kept saying.

Eventually Lois closed her eyes and Miranda put a blanket on her and left as well.

By the time she got back to the guest apartment Dave was very drunk.

"Quite the shindig," he said. "Quite the party."

Miranda could think of nothing to say.

"Makes me miss being alone," said Dave and opened another bottle of expensive wine.

"Pour me a glass too," said Miranda and he did.

It was very dark beyond the reflection of the candles in the windows. They could see the occasional flare of fire out at the refinery where the diggers were working.

"You know," said Miranda. "I think I saw the Dog-Killing Goat Boy once, driving a motorbike down a highway in western Pennsylvania."

"Jesus Christ, Miranda," said Dave. "I made all that shit up. I was taking the piss out of those pompous motherfuckers."

"Still," said Miranda. "Wish I had left him some ciggies and liquor."

"Jesus Christ."

4

DAVE WAS HUNGOVER THE NEXT DAY, and surly, so Miranda went to visit Lois. They sat quietly in the living room waiting for the kettle on the Coleman stove to whistle and stared out the window at the huge blue sky. The sun was a shimmering concentration of light hovering slightly over the horizon and the world looked tired and pale. When they finally had their tea, Miranda asked Lois for the second time how she was doing and the older woman began to cry.

"I'm OK," she finally said. "I have no right to be surprised, but I am. Something like this was going to happen eventually, of course it did, it happens to everyone, doesn't it? But who can ever be prepared?"

She looked out the window.

"It would be easier, I think," she continued, "if we had known each other before, if he had been my first husband, if our lives had been more entangled. It feels a little like I made friends with someone sitting beside me on a bus, a nice gentleman, someone sweet and kind, and then before we got to our destination he had a stroke and now everyone on the bus expects me to take care of him because we were sitting beside each other and we liked each other. Everyone on the bus is staring at me like it's my problem, my issue."

"How long have you known each other?"

"Five years," said Lois and then looked sharply at Miranda: "I know it sounds like a long time, but it's not. Not really. Relationships don't have weight anymore, they don't have permanence. They aren't something you are in, like they were, you aren't in relationships, you have relations, nothing fixed, nothing meaningful, nothing with a name, there is the person you are talking to in that instance, in that moment, nobody else matters because nobody else is really there, nobody else looks at your relationships and thinks: siblings, married, mother-daughter, parent-child, because those categories have been shown to be entirely empty. Nobody cares, no one watches you, no one judges you, no one measures themselves against you. Even in a place like this where we are crammed together, everyone always looks the other way at the last minute. They always turn and look away because they can't bear the meaninglessness of what your relationships say about the meaninglessness of theirs. It's all empty of significance to anyone other than yourself which means it's empty of significance altogether. You can do anything you want now: anything."

Miranda glanced through the windows at the incandescent sky.

"I could kill him," said Lois. "I could kill him and no one would care."

They sat quietly and sipped their tea. Lois stood up and went into the kitchen. Miranda could hear her crying. Down the hall their bedroom door was open and Miranda could see Franz's feet on the bed on top of the covers, black dress socks still on. Miranda put her cup down and walked to the front door. She turned to tell Lois she would be back later, to thank her for the tea.

Lois was staring at her: hair a mess, eyes bloodshot and bulging, like blisters about to pop.

"Why couldn't he have just died?" she said. "Why is he still alive? Why? Why?"

Miranda walked down the hall past all the closed doors: all the doors that belonged to all the former professors and former architects and former teachers and assorted former-something-else's and all the doors for which she had no occupational labels but in theory once contained human beings who formerly held jobs. Were they all empty? The rooms without names? Without labels? Were they cells in which these formerly employed people had bricked themselves in? Were they prisons for the redundant? Were they crypts? Mausoleums? She thought of cliff burials in China and deserted nests under barn eaves and empty cocoons glued to branches by extruded cements, she thought of advent calendars and how, when she was small, the blank faces of unopened days gave her a thrill of fear.

The stairwell smelled of damp concrete, bare bulbs hung from the ceiling like sacks of insect eggs. The steps were a little too shallow and Miranda skipped down them. She counted the floors one by one, cycling through the right angles. She thought about going all the way down into the basements and sub-basements and past them, right down into the earth, to disappear, to dissolve into soil and darkness, but instead she exited the stairs into the massive glass and steel husk of the building's mall. The dust in the air provided a medium in which the shafts of morning light could manifest and she felt her insignificance: a little figure inked into the corner, an element of a nineteenth-century engraving of an Oriental edifice, only there to provide the gentlemen back home with a sense of scale.

Mel and the kids were outside. The oldest was digging up Eli's peonies and the youngest crawling around in the muck. Mel sat on the bench watching them, housecoat pulled tight around her, pajama legs tightly crossed, feet in mangy slippers.

"Oh, hi Miranda." She scooched down the bench and Miranda sat beside her. "How was the party?"

"Greg didn't tell you?"

"He told me you were there and you looked fantastic."

"He didn't mention Franz collapsing."

"No," said Mel. "He mostly talked about you. And he said your friend irritated Adrian by telling a long strange story about a goat man. Greg was pretty pleased about it. He doesn't much care for Adrian."

"Franz had a massive stroke," said Miranda.

Mel shrugged.

"What's your friend's name?" she asked. "I can never remember names."

"Dave," said Miranda.

"Are you guys together?"

"We're traveling together."

"But are you together together?"

"No."

"I didn't think so, but Greg thought you might be."

"No. We're not together together."

"You don't have any weed, do you? I could smell it on you guys the other day."

The baby started to cry and Mel scooped the child up.

"Sorry," said Miranda. "But I'm sure Dave can set you up."

"That's OK," Mel was bouncing the child on her knee. "I just haven't smoked any for so long. Greg is against weed, and Adrian, everyone around here is, but sometimes I miss it and Greg said your friend was a pothead."

"Dave," said Miranda. "His name is Dave."

"Dave," said Mel. The baby's fat cheeks were smeared with dirt and tears and snot. "Dave, with whom you are not together together."

"Yes," said Miranda. "That Dave."

The older child put something in his mouth and chewed on it thoughtfully.

"Greg wants to fuck you," Mel did not take her eyes of the baby. "I can tell from the way he talks about you, looks at you."

"You have nothing to fear in that regard," said Miranda.

Mel laughed.

"I wouldn't mind," she said. "If you wanted to. It would get him off my case. I get tired of fighting him off."

"Still," said Miranda. "I'd rather not."

"Really?" said Mel and spoke to the infant in her baby voice. "He's a nice-looking guy, don't you think? A nice-looking guy! A nice-looking guy!"

"Sure," said Miranda. "Nice-looking guy. You're lucky to have him. Seems like a good dad."

"Oh, he's not the father of my kids," said Mel.

"No?"

"I would never have a baby with him, not with a regular, not with a survivor. He's nice to have around, and I like him, but he's damaged goods. He's filled with corruption, like all the others around here. That's why they're here and not digging: something wrong inside, in their heads, in all of them. That's why the virus or whatever couldn't get them, they were already broken things, diseased. I would never pass that on, what all these men have, pollution. I would never have a child with Greg."

"Oh," said Miranda.

Mel gave her a sidelong glance, blue eyes behind blonde hair. "I had a dream," Mel said and smiled a little smile. "I had a dream. My children and my children's children, and their children too, like the stars in the sky. Just like in the Bible: stars in the sky. I had a dream."

The older child began to cry and Mel put the baby down. It slumped forward onto its hands, fingers curling like caterpillars.

"I would never let one of these sad losers impregnate me," Mel said. "Never. The thought disgusts me. If something got stuck in me I would tear it out. So if you want to fuck Greg, you go ahead. You go right ahead. I don't care. I'm pretty much done with that end of things anyway. Once in a while it's nice to mess around, but I don't thinks it's really worth it anymore, worth the trouble, worth the risk. If you think about it rationally. Frankly, it would be a blessing to have one less thing to worry about."

Miranda found a deer path winding through the chaotic green fringe of the river. She followed as the trail wound between old factories and past strange utilitarian structures lost in the rubble, past fungal intersections of steel pipes, copulatory tangles of rebar, PVC, and climbing plants, hunched over trees consuming fragments of chain link fences. The path finally spilled out onto an old river walk. On the far side of the Maumee she saw deserted docks, warehouses, and clustered trees in silhouette, an undifferentiated dark mass in the early morning shade, but up above that featureless gloom rose glittering scaffolding, white concrete chimneys and rusting water towers that shone in the sun.

Miranda picked her way towards a bridge, slipping and sliding in the slick mud, grasping at crooked branches and skinny young trees. She stopped at the massive concrete abutments and examined the fading graffiti, looked up at the black stippling on the underbelly, listened to the water rushing past, imagined how once it would have sounded in stereo, with vehicles pouring back and forth overhead. On the other side of the water a black dog came trotting into view, nose down, and she thought of all the land between Toledo and the Appalachians, alive with half-wild things and feral ecologies. It looked like it was tracking something, jamming its nose into the sulfurous muck under leaves, into crevasses and little gullies. It stopped when it was directly opposite and stared straight at her. Its eyes did not appear to be yellow but it was hard to tell. It lost interest in her almost instantly and continued on its way.

Miranda started scrambling back up to the city level and found a cement staircase wedged into the joint of bridge and soil. She climbed past broken bottles, crushed beer cans, an old shoe, until she emerged on a curving road. She could see the Co-op tower rising up a few blocks away. She turned her back on it and crossed the mouth of the bridge, glancing down its empty expanse, noting it was cleared and maintained for the passage of the tanker trucks. She kept walking down the curving road towards Lake Erie until she came to the marina.

She found Eli and spent the afternoon with him. They sat on the steps of the building he occupied, staring out at the river and the industrial pandemonium across the way, at the barely visible daemonic flickering of the refinery fires. A tanker docked and the diggers were preparing to pump it dry, to suck all the thick, granular crude into the tangled pipes, tanks, and organs of the massive machine in which it would be sweetened and purified. Miranda could barely pick out the little figures crawling about on the rusting shell of the ship. Eli grilled her fresh fish and bannock on a hibachi and they drank high-proof home brew from mason jars.

"Why do you make your own?" asked Miranda.

Eli shrugged.

"So much of it still lying around," said Miranda. "There for the taking."

"Well, it's not a point of principle," said Eli. "Never had much time for principles."

They sat in silence for a while.

"It's something to do," said Eli. "Not that I'm bored. I just like it. The process. I like paying attention to something. Thinking about it. It's a hobby, I suppose, like what those folks up at the tower have."

"They don't have hobbies," said Miranda. "Those folks have art. And culture. And principles."

Eli laughed.

"They getting under your skin already?"

"I suppose they are," said Miranda. "I don't know why. They're harmless."

"Nobody is harmless," said Eli. "Especially not nobodies with principles."

The sun crawled to its zenith and sank, the sky darkening, the intricate chaos of industry on the opposite bank resolving back into a dense black unity. They could see the shimmering heat of the coals in the hibachi, the mottling embers. Eli threw some venison sausages on the grill and found a bottle of white wine. Soon they were burning their fingers on the blistered sausage and washing the steaming globules of meat down with wine. The coagulate stars blotted out the void above them. Miranda thought of Mel and her dream, she thought of her dense little body, of blue veins beneath white skin, agar jelly, she thought of yeast, fermentation, of windblown mold inseminating milky cheese.

5

"ELI?" MIRANDA HAD JUST TOLD GREG where she spent the previous day. Greg had shot a pig and Miranda was helping him gut and clean it in a supermarket across the street from the tower. Most of the shelves were cleaned out, but there was a butcher's counter and equipment in the back those few folks in the tower who hunted liked to use.

"That crazy old motherfucker," They split the carcass and

Greg cut out the tenderloin and was trimming the belly back to get at the ham. "Adrian hates him."

"Is there anyone Adrian doesn't hate?" Miranda asked and Greg laughed.

"I don't think so," said Greg. "Maybe himself. But even that's probably love-hate more than love-love."

He straightened up and wiped sweat from his brow, leaving a streak of blood and grime across his forehead.

"I don't know if Adrian has anything at all to do with Eli leaving, really," he said. "But he didn't help. Eli used to be a big artist or something, so Adrian was infatuated with him for a while. Used to harass him all the time. Try to get him to do his sculptures or whatever. But Eli was done with that shit. It made Adrian crazy. He would go on and on about wasted talent. How talented people had a duty to humanity. Total bullshit, but he would go on and on about it. Then when Adrian finally gave up trying to get the man to do what he wanted, and Eli had some peace and quiet, he did start working on something again."

"Adrian must have been delighted."

"He was." Greg stopped talking while he cut the muscle open to the bone. It was white and damp as a shoot emerging from the soil.

"Pass me the saw," he said.

"I'll do it," said Miranda. Greg shrugged.

Her shoulder started throbbing as soon as she began and she remembered the spill from her bike in Pennsylvania. The buttressed church and the crow and the billboard. Greg wiped his hands off on a filthy towel while he watched.

"So Adrian was pretty excited, and he began to pester Eli about what he was up to, but Eli wouldn't let anyone into his apartment, even though we all knew he was up to something because he was hidden away up there for hours and hours, and we could hear banging and crashing and he was throwing rubbish out his windows, and lugging a lot of shit down the stairs to dump out behind the building as well. But he wouldn't tell us what it was he was doing. Adrian espoused all kinds of theories.

Made all kinds of speeches. Gave lectures on the future of art, in anticipation of the first significant piece of post-event work to be created by an important artist."

The bone flecks fell on Miranda's hands in a mist. The whizz-whizz-whizz of the saw was satisfying, the friction, the tug of the bone against the steel.

"Then when he was finally done, Eli left. One morning he didn't come down, and then the next, and the next, until we realized he wasn't going to reappear and so a bunch of us went up to see if he was okay, and the door was open and he was gone."

"At least Adrian got his work of art," she said and the saw slipped through the last shards of the bone.

"He sure did," laughed Greg.

Miranda looked at him quizzically.

"Go up and see yourself. Room 709."

On the way back to the tower Miranda came across Adrian working in his little garden. He was weeding the perfect rows of seedlings.

"Oh, hi Miranda," he said and straightened up. "What have you been up to? You look terrible."

"Butchering a pig," she said.

Adrian grimaced.

"With Greg?" he asked and Miranda nodded.

"What a queer couple they are," he said as she started to leave. She stopped.

"Greg and Mel," he said.

"Especially Mel," he continued. "Greg's rough around the edges and a little over-aggressive, but Mel's genuinely idiosyncratic, strange ideas about the world, strange attitude, all disconnected."

He cleared his throat and waited for Miranda to say something, but she didn't.

"Rumor has it," said Adrian, "when things first went weird and there were a lot of left over kids hanging about downtown, before they wandered off to the docks or out into the country or wherever they went, she used to take the older boys up to her apartment, the ones just reaching puberty. She would take them up there one at a time when Greg was out hunting and scavenging."

Adrian grimaced again.

"But those are rumors," he said. "And one mustn't judge even if they are true. Things aren't like they used to be, are they?"

"No," said Miranda. "I suppose they are not."

"And poor Mel," he said. "She has some strange ideas about the provenance of those children, about what exactly a gene pool is and what keeps it healthy. Very dedicated to the propagation of our species but not well-educated, our Mel, fertile of body and imagination, but not well-educated: trash, really."

In the afternoon, Dave and Miranda went to Greg and Mel's for tenderloin medallions and spring potatoes. Greg was pretty drunk by the time they got there and was bitching about Adrian.

"That guy drives everyone off," he said and splashed Johnnie Walker into their tumblers.

Mel was at a Coleman stove, searing the medallions in the pig's fat with rosemary and garlic. The kids were clinging to her feet.

"Oh yeah?" said Dave. "Who did he drive off?"

"Eli, for one," said Greg and waved his tumbler at Miranda. "Room 709."

Dave looked at her with a raised eyebrow and she shrugged.

"There was a librarian who used to live here who argued with him all the time. About politics of all things. About politics in the long ago. Fucking insane. The whole world gone mad and they would argue about Hillary fucking Clinton. She finally got sick of his shit and left."

"How did you feel about Hillary?" asked Dave and Greg stared at him.

"What?"

"About Hillary." Dave was wearing his serious taking-the-piss face. "How did you feel about her?"

"It doesn't fucking matter. It was years ago. It was old before this shit happened. It's dead politics. Dead politicians. Dead." He stared hard at Dave and raised his voice. "It doesn't fucking matter!"

"Take it easy, Greg," said Mel and splashed white wine into the hissing, sizzling pan. There was a burst of dizzying aroma.

"I am taking it easy," said Greg to Mel. "What do I think of Hillary fucking Clinton? This guy. You joking?"

"Sure," said Dave. "Making a joke."

Greg shook his head.

"Anyway," he said. "He drove her off, the librarian. And Eli. And that guy, that financial advisor with the shakes, and the doctor. The epidemiologist or whatever. Really useful to have a doctor around, but Adrian drove her off with his constant nattering on about community health and developing our own vaccinations and how do we plan a really healthy diet."

"Are you sure, hon?" said Mel from the kitchen. "Adrian didn't drive the doctor off, did he?"

"Yes he fucking did," said Greg.

"I thought she died?"

"What?"

"She died, didn't she?"

"No, she fucking didn't. She left and said she was going to look for her kids in Florida."

"Really?" Mel frowned in confusion. "I thought it was the nutritionist who went to Florida. And she was looking for her Mom."

Greg stared at her, eyes wide, mouth tight, and poured himself another tumbler full of whiskey.

When Mel served the food, Greg insisted on getting up and walking around the table to sit next to Miranda so they could continue their conversation about Adrian. He kept pressing his leg against hers under the table.

"He likes you well enough," said Greg to Miranda and then swung his head heavily towards Dave. "But he doesn't like you."

Mel was dishing out the potatoes and fussing over portion

size.

"Why's that?" asked Dave. "Why doesn't Adrian like me?"

He opened a bottle of wine and was pouring big glasses out for him and Miranda.

"You're black," said Greg.

"Oh?" said Dave. "I thought he didn't like me because I so transparently don't like him."

"No," said Greg. "That's not why he doesn't like you. He doesn't like you because you are black. And he is a racist."

"A racist?" said Mel. "Adrian?"

She sat down and everyone except Greg picked up their cutlery.

"The doctor he chased off was black," Greg said. "Wasn't she?"

"I could have sworn the doctor died," said Mel. "Go ahead and eat, everyone. I thought it was the nutritionist he drove off. Wasn't it the nutritionist? The white nutritionist?"

Greg got up unsteadily. Dave and Miranda tucked in.

"No, Mel, you got it all wrong. Again. It was the doctor, but it doesn't matter. It doesn't fucking matter who was white and who was black. It doesn't matter who left and who stayed and died. None of it fucking matters except that fucking Adrian is a smug fucking racist fucking cunt," he said. "I'll crack another bottle."

"And this is a fucking delicious fucking meal, Mel," said Dave cheerfully.

Mel laughed but Greg simply blinked.

After Greg passed out on the couch and the kids were napping in their rooms, Mel asked Dave if he had weed and he rolled a big fat bomber for them to share.

"Greg's against weed," Mel said. "He thinks it's unhealthy. He thinks it's decadent. He thinks it gets into your DNA. He thinks it was drugs that messed everything up. It screwed up the copies, the human copies, they ruined everything."

"Really?" said Dave. "He's blaming the weed? What was he before? Was he a cop?"

Mel laughed.

"He likes to pretend he was," she said. "But who knows. Everyone around here is always pretending things. Making up stories. I don't really care. I don't much listen when he talks about the past."

Dave lit up.

"Actually," she added. "I don't much listen to him at all. I don't much listen to anyone."

"Is that right?" said Dave. "I'm pretty sure Miranda doesn't either."

Mel laughed again.

Miranda grabbed the Johnnie Walker, a candle, and some matches from the kitchen, and left the two of them by the open window watching the waves of heat rise from the overgrown city, their feet up on the window sill, handing the joint back and forth.

The hallways on the seventh floor were thick with dust and cobwebs and the flickering candlelight made the walls look like they were moving, sliding about. Miranda felt a twist of anxiety, and suddenly saw the passage she was in as a shaft carved out of living stone, as part of a catacomb, as something buried, and the absurdity of the thought relaxed her.

The door of 709 was a little stiff but when she leaned into it, it popped abruptly open. Wind and light washed over her, for a moment in indistinguishable solidarity, and she gasped at the surprise of it. Her candle had blown out but she didn't notice, just held it in her hand and stared. The interior walls of the apartment were knocked out, and the exterior wall of windows too, where the floor-to-ceiling glass had once been there was now clearly a large, square section of blue sky, out of which all that energy was pouring into the room.

After she blinked the light and the wind out of her eyes, she realized every square inch of walls, floor and ceiling had been carved into a maze of grooves. She knelt down and touched the surface. The concrete was cool, the grooves about half an inch deep and polished smooth. She walked gingerly into the space, as if the carving might crumble under her weight. She ran her hand along the wall, feeling the texture as waves, as spasms, as the undulations of a cold animal. Something alive and moving and inhuman. She walked to the edge and peered out, a seagull turned below her, the cars deserted on the bridge, shivering bursts of ripples on the brown river, the long eastward shadow of the tower cutting across the boundaries of earth and water, tree and building.

She sat down, legs dangling over the edge, feeling the whiskey and the wine tightening her temples, feeling – distantly – the tremble of euphoria, feeling it in the goose-pimple crawl of her skin, feeling it in the laughing quiver of her breath. She thought of Eli doing all the work, all the labour this would have taken. She sat there for a long time, drinking out of the bottle, watching the shadow of the building grow and soften, its hard edges mellowing, spreading across the land. The sky became engorged with vivid blues and reds and purples as the sun sank in the west, somewhere behind the building, behind her.

6

IT WAS MIRANDA'S TURN TO NURSE a hangover but Dave didn't care.

"Come on, sleepyhead," he said. "Let's get out of here."

"What do you mean?"

"This place is horrible," said Dave. "It's a tomb, a crypt, a mausoleum. Let's leave."

"OK," said Miranda. "Tomorrow."

"Today."

"Why are you so chipper?" asked Miranda "Where's your headache?"

"Where's my headache?" mimicked Dave. "Where's my nausea? Where's my sickness of the soul? My despair? My ennui?"

He fired up the camp stove in the kitchen and brought instant coffee to her in bed.

And a plate of bacon and eggs.

And more coffee.

"You'll be dead soon enough," he said, "along with everyone else, and the universe will be drained entirely of your subjectivity, of our subjectivity, of all subjectivity, and no one will ever have to notice anything ever again, listen to anyone ever again, suffer the consequences of their decisions ever again. No one will ever be hungover again. You can rest then, in soothing annihilation, but now you are young and alive, and you can see the world in your sickness: enjoy the world in your sickness: love the world in your sickness: love the glorious, glorious world."

"Ok," said Miranda. "Ok. Let's leave. I'll go with you. If you shut up I'll come along. Just stop talking to me. Please stop talking at me."

Dave grinned.

"And stop smiling at me."

Dave stopped.

"And stop looking at me."

She threw a pillow at him.

Dave began carting the empty water jugs up to the roof, filling them from the rainwater barrels and lugging them back down, replacing all they had used in their brief stay.

"Give me a minute and I'll help you out." Miranda was up and washing the dishes.

"No worries, kiddo, almost done," he said. "Two more trips."

"Where's all this energy coming from?"

"I'm tired of these angsty bourgeois refugees fussing about their social status," said Dave. "It's exhausting. It's like they failed entirely to notice no one gives a fuck about them anymore, they do not matter, they never did."

"When I left last night you and Mel were getting high, and Greg was face down on the couch making noises like he was due to puke," said Miranda. "And I have to be honest, it didn't look like angsty bourgeois refugees fussing about their social status."

Dave laughed, "Mel, what a nutty kid. You ever talk to her? Batshit crazy, but in an interesting way, you know? The rest of them, though, garden-variety neurotics, dime-a-dozen, dull, dull, dull. Horrifying to think they're what's left of civilization."

And then he was gone.

After she washed the dishes, Miranda straightened up the apartment and stole a few bars of soap from the bathroom. Dave was already downstairs in the van and had insisted Miranda take the apartment keys to Adrian because he didn't want to have to interact with the man. She locked the door behind her and looked up to see Greg peering at her from the open door of his apartment.

"Hey, Greg," she said. "What's going on?"

He was sickly pale.

"I've been throwing up all morning," he said.

"I'm not surprised," said Miranda. "You were sure putting it back last night."

"Have you seen Mel?" he asked. "Or the kids?"

"No," said Miranda. "We've been packing up."

"You're leaving?" Greg almost groaned. "Was it last night? Was it because of last night?"

"What? No. No. Last night was lovely."

Greg stared at her.

"Fun," she said. "It was fun."

"It was a fucking train wreck," he said. "It was fucking awful."

"Mel," he said, voice breaking, and stared straight into her eyes. "Mel."

The twenty feet of carpeted hallway between them was endless insurmountable wilderness.

He slammed the door.

She walked down the empty hall past the apartment and climbed the stairs to Adrian's floor. When she got to his apartment, she knocked. There was no answer. She put her ear against it and heard nothing. She tried the handle and it swung open. The early afternoon light was pouring through the windows. Ella's chair was empty. An open bottle of wine was on the marble island; two wine glasses – one empty, one full. Miranda walked quietly over and put the keys to the guest suite down beside the bottle. She heard a moan from the hall and looked up. The bedroom door was open and through it, she could see a mirror. At first she saw only her own startled face but when she looked away from the mirror to the bed, she saw Ella lying there, watching her, mouth flaccid. Adrian was on top of her, the muscles along the crease of his spine straining, his neck arched. He moaned again and Ella's arm fell heavily off the edge of the bed, opening up so Miranda could see the pale flash of her inner elbow. The thumb, index, and forefingers relaxed, pointing more-or-less to the floor, the other two fingers slightly curled. The black dress – the pencil dress, the Alexander McQueen – was a pool of black on the floor next to the bed.

Dave was leaning against the van smoking a joint and watching Lois at work in her garden. Mel was on her usual bench, staring up at the sky, arms stretched out across the back of it, legs crossed, one pointed toe gently bouncing, the kids at her feet. Otherwise, the common space was empty.

"You give him the keys?" Dave asked.

"Sure," said Miranda and walked to the driver's side.

"Did he say anything?" Dave dropped the joint and stepped on it.

"No. He was busy. Left them on the table."

"I couldn't bring myself to like him," said Dave, opened the door, and slid in.

"In fact," he said as Miranda got in and started the motor, "I think I actually hate the smug little prick."

"I don't much care for him either," said Miranda.

Mel and Lois looked up as the motor started but the kids kept playing. Dave gave them a languid wave. Mel returned the wave but Lois merely stared. As they drove off Miranda watched them diminish in the rearview mirror. Lois returned to her work. Mel let her head fall lazily back and gazed up at the empty sky. Miranda could practically feel the weight of the day's heat against the other woman's body, the perspiration on the tight skin of her forehead, of her breastbone, feel the swell of her ribs as her lungs filled with the golden light that poured down between the buildings and crashed silently about her. As the two human figures dwindled into insignificance in the mirror, the skyscrapers and office blocks around them seemed to briefly swell, the myriad windows catching the sun and the sky in a splintering flash of light and color, before they too were reduced to an unremarkable irregularity on the horizon.

IV

THE WEST

1

THEY SAW THE BICYCLIST WHEN THEY were on the outskirts of Chicago. They were driving across the crest of a massive concrete arch, weaving slowly between the deserted vehicles, and Miranda was observing the stands of weeds and wildflowers, the mildewed patches of black and ochre and rust that were beginning their slow deconstruction of the thing, when Dave interrupted her reverie.

"Hey, look at that."

On the highway running beneath them was what looked like a scuttling beetle, all crooked limbs and darting movement, whirring between the lanes of motionless vehicles. It took a second to distinguish the pumping knees and the bobbing head and the elbows all-askew from the whirring wheels and the handlebars and the little wagon hauled behind. The figure passed underneath them and was gone.

"What do you think?" asked Dave.

"What do I think?"

"Yeah, what do you think? Should we go say hi?"

Miranda frowned.

"Come on," said Dave. "Let's go say hello. They can tell us what's going on in the city. What's happening. What's up."

At the next exit, Miranda swung the car off the overpass and slung it around the long curving ramp onto the southward road.

They gained on the cyclist rapidly but were stymied by a cluster of cars parked diagonally across their path. Dave hopped out of the van.

"Hey!" he shouted. "Hey!"

And then Miranda leaned on the horn.

Tonya sat cross-legged beside a hibachi, in a little grotto made by the abandoned vehicles. Dave was frying up some chops he acquired from Mel and Greg on the evening of their little party. Miranda was leaning against the van.

"There's no one making pharmaceuticals in Chicago," said Tonya. She was a small wiry woman, late fifties or early sixties, leathered face, grey hair cropped short.

"Really?" Dave turned the chops. "But I heard from numerous people. Numerous sources. Some guy is at the University of Chicago making anti-psychotics, anti-seizure meds. Lotsa folks told me."

"No one up there now," said Tonya. "Just the kids."

"Just the kids," repeated Dave and a tic rolled across his face.

They listened to the meat sizzle and Dave began to craft a joint.

"You want a glass of wine or anything?" he asked and she shook her head.

When he was lit up he offered her a hit and she shook her head again.

"So what were you doing up there?" Dave asked.

"Just passing through," said the woman.

"Yeah," said Dave. "Just passing through. Now I guess we are too."

The sun went down by the time they finished eating and Dave retired to the van. Miranda was now cross-legged by the hibachi as well.

"I'm sorry I disappointed your friend," said Tonya.

"Ah well," said Miranda. "If it wasn't you that disappointed him today, it would have been reality tomorrow."

Tonya's smile was barely visible in the late evening light.

"Reality? Am I something unreal?" she asked. "Am I a ghost to you?"

"Well, you aren't a digger," said Miranda. "So you might as well be."

The coals were still glowing in the hibachi and the stars were out.

"What were you doing in Chicago?" Miranda asked.

"Visiting the kids," said Tonya.

They sat in silence for a few minutes.

Tonya got up, dug around in her bicycle trailer and pulled out some boxes of Maxi-pads and condoms before she found her sleeping bag and a tightly rolled foam mattress. She glanced at Miranda.

"They aren't for me," she said.

Miranda returned her calm stare.

"The kids," Tonya said. "I like to look in on them. Place to place. It gives me something to do. They don't know anything do they?"

"I guess not," said Miranda.

"Especially now that the older ones, the ones who remember more clearly how things were before, have started joining the diggers."

She repacked the condoms and the Maxi-pads.

"I hand stuff like this out," she continued. "Explain what it's for, where to find it. Explain the facts of life. Because most of them have got a few years of puberty before the other change hits them, the big one, before they get the call to go out to the diggings. A couple of years is a long time when you're young. A long time to be frightened and ignorant and, God bless them, sometimes pregnant. So I give them some sex ed. Tell them what's what. Show them how to use this stuff. And diapers. They'll never run out of the gear if they're near a town. They'll all be dead first or digging before they run out of what they need. But they don't know anything, so I explain it all as best I can. Then when I'm done my spiel, I move on to the next town."

She laid out the foam and the sleeping bag next to the Hibachi and climbed in. In a few minutes she was snoring. Miranda looked up at the stars, picking out the constellations she remembered from her childhood, from late nights in the winter, out with her dad, their breath hanging in the air, snow creaking under their boots, out on some country road where the lights didn't get in the way. Mom at home making hot chocolate. Those were the years before the big fights. Before the teenage angst. Before the inevitable disappointments of learning who her parents were, who she was. Not that she was ever nostalgic for childhood. Not even now. It was part of the continuing sequence of events into which she had been flung: days and nights, waking up and falling asleep, getting hungry and finding food. She never trusted memories, the emotions and feelings that adhered arbitrarily to the uneven topographies of desire, mere accumulations, growths, strange semi-conscious intensities. It was easy enough to organize one's life into skeletal abstractions, to build a narrative of this and then that and then this, but such rationalizations were as frail as fish bones, constructions that contained very little of life as it was actually lived, the life that was a constant wash of energy over and through the body.

"First we lived near Gramma in Philadelphia in the apartment near the park where the dogs would be," Miranda murmured to herself. "Then Dad got the job in Minnesota and we drove with the trailer and stayed in motels with chlorinated pools, then I started school and peed myself and made friends and got grades and went sledding and had sleepovers, then Mom got her degree while I watched TV and Dad heated soup, then Mom got her job and I went to high school and learned how to drink beer and smoke weed and mess around and in the summers we would go to the cottage and water skiing and diving off the dock and sunburns so bad you had to sleep with the sheets off, and then I graduated and visited Gramma on my own and got a job in the bar and would fall asleep on her couch on Sundays, then college and summer jobs and boring boring boring, and then the trip to Europe across the ocean in the plane and coming home after at least a million years of evolution but nothing changed at all, everything was exactly the same as before, and then college again and summer jobs and boring boring boring, and then a career in New York City and money and clothes and drinking coffee and trying to have fun and trying to live and be someone and do things, and Mom and Dad visited, and then the digging started, and then I went to Philadelphia to look for Gramma and wait for Mom and Dad, but they never came, so then to Baltimore to look for Mom's folks, and then to Florida, and then back to Philadelphia, and walking and walking and walking and then driving driving driving with Dave and now we're here, just outside Chicago, and then I'm going to look for Mom and Dad but they'll be dead or gone digging, because they would have come to check on Gramma and me, but they didn't. And then I'll be done."

She got up and walked to the edge of the road, hopped over the abutment and walked down a side street. It was old shops and small apartment blocks, the cracked pavement completely overwhelmed by the undergrowth and the stars obscured by the trees. It was dark, like being underground, like being in a cave, she could barely see where she was stepping but there was a sort of pleasure in it, in the density of the darkness. She closed her eyes and walked a few feet more before she opened them and turned around to walk back. She saw movement beyond the trees, something flashing across the face of an apartment, something with limbs akimbo, a bobbing head. The distorted shadow of a dog, she told herself, or a coyote. She walked briskly back to the main road, clambered back over the abutment, but paused, squatting for a long while in the deep shadows outside their little camp, until she heard the sad, moaning howl of a coyote or a big dog.

In the morning, Tonya was gone and Dave wanted to sleep so they stuck around for another day.

In the evening, after they ate, Dave hauled out all his notebooks, maybe a half dozen of them, and tore the pages out one by one, slowly and painstakingly burning them in the hibachi. Miranda caught glimpses of lists, long scrawling paragraphs, sketches of people and structures, diagrams – all crumpled up, set alight in the tender flames, transformed into black ash. When he was done, Dave leaned back against the wheel of the van and rolled a joint. His hands were trembling.

"So what next?" he asked.

"You don't want to go up into Chicago?"

"What's the point? It's going to be a zoo. All those savage little children, savage little motherfuckers running around, armed to the teeth with all those leftover handguns, AR-15s, hand grenades stolen from army bases, smashed on peppermint liqueurs, Old Baileys, fighting over half-looted supermarkets and warehouses full of canned beans."

"Is that how you imagine them? I always think of Peter Pan's lost boys. But with girls."

"Anyways," said Dave. "I'm not going up there to waste my time."

"Waste your time?" Miranda asked. "You're worried about time now?"

"Tick tick tick," said Dave and tapped his forefinger against his temple with every tick. "It could all blow up at any moment."

"She might be full of shit, you know, about Chicago."

"Did she strike you as the type of woman who tells frivolous lies?"

"No," said Miranda. "She did not."

"She did not seem that way to me either," said Dave and then, "Do you mind if I tag along? When you go looking for your people?"

"I thought you wanted to go out west?"

"It's on the way, isn't it? You said Minnesota."

"That's what I said."

"That's OK. That's fine by me. Love to see all those northern lakes and forests."

Miranda shrugged.

"And then you can come with me after," said Dave. "Out onto the Prairies. See Wounded Knee. The Black Hills. That Crazy Horse memorial. See the Rockies."

"Unless my folks are still there."

"Yeah," said Dave, his face contorted with a massive twitch. "Of course, if your folks are still there."

2

IT WAS PRETTY QUIET the next day. Dave sat with his legs drawn up, feet on the dashboard, and stared out the window. Miranda listened to the hum of the engine, the pitch changes when she shifted through the gears. The highways were wide open and clear and the diggings were vast and empty, but the trucks kept rolling by, convoys from Milwaukee or Duluth. She watched the horizon as she drove, looking for the clouds of dust that indicated diggers at work, but there was nothing.

"Depopulation," Dave said at midmorning. "Depredation. Desolation."

"Diminution," said Miranda, and he laughed.

He fell asleep shortly after and groaned: deep heartbroken moans, mournful, shameful, and she glanced at him. He was leaning against the window, knees pulled up to his chest, hands clasped underneath his head for a pillow. She was struck, for the first time, by how smooth his skin was, and how long his lashes, the lips full and half open. He looked younger asleep than she imagined him. She could see him as a boy, almost, not quite, but almost, or perhaps it wasn't his childhood she saw in him but his children, perhaps that was what he was dreaming of, of his kids, perhaps she saw them shining through his skin, their ghosts, the memories of them, trying to be free of him, trying to escape the containment of his grief and disperse, trying to sublimate, it was a word he used before, that he liked: sublimate. She thought about his claim he was only alive out of a stubborn curiosity, and she considered perhaps it was not curiosity at all, but pure stubbornness, a refusal to accept what happened to him really happened, a refusal to let the old things die, the old ways of thinking and being and doing. His memories of how things were grew inside of him, were consuming him, they superseded the actual events of the past. Of the present. She imagined his tics and twitches and seizures were not the false starts and stops of his nervous system but something else entirely, evidence of necromancy, of demonic pacts. It was not only Dave she saw in those moments but the people he had captured, whom he still possessed, the people inside him: his phantom wife, his phantom lovers, parents, children, shifting around, moving, restless, waiting for him to die so they could cast him aside and be done with this, done with Dave, the last of their dreary human forms.

The diggings ceased abruptly right before Rockford and the thick tidal bush surged up to the roads. It was a wilderness, but the telephone and power lines and street signs and tops of office blocks and apartments and lampposts and fast food joints and all manner of other feral signifiers let you know it was something else once, briefly, something that was seized with a fitful, intermittent sort of a self-awareness and was now drifting back into annihilation.

Miranda thought suddenly of Ella, sitting in her chair in the well-appointed apartment – elegantly dressed, her makeup perfect, staring blankly out the window. She tried to remember if she had looked into Ella's eyes when they were introduced, if she noticed their color, if she had watched to see her pupils dilate.

She thought of Mel on the bench, her children at her feet, the sunlight settling on her like a beautiful shroud.

She thought of Mary after Arthur beat her, curled up in her clean white sheets, staring at the wall, finished with it all.

She thought of herself, closing Esther's apartment door behind her, gliding down the stairs, out of the apartment, out into the world.

Dave was awake when she came back from a pee, twisting and stretching in his seat, sullen with sleep.

"No more cities," he said. "I can't stand them anymore. They're grotesque."

"The roads might not be as clear if we get off the big highways."

"No more cities," said Dave.

"Alright," said Miranda. "We'll cross the Mississippi just before Madison and cut south of Minneapolis."

"Wake me up before we leave this main drag," said Dave. "And I'll show you how to acquire gas."

Then he rolled over and closed his eyes.

Miranda dug around in the back for some food and found a can of chickpeas. She poured out the liquid, ate a couple of spoonfuls, and brought it up front with her to snack on while she drove.

There was the dark lump of a dead bear on the side of the road. A hairy growth, a tumor erupting from beneath the concrete skin. Miranda slowed down but she could identify no single feature: no distinct limbs, no clawed paws, no dead eyes or fixed snarling maw. It was an inert mass of fur, muscle and fat.

Her father told her a story once, about when he was building the cottage they owned up north, on a lake right on the Canadian border, and how one night, when the walls were already up, and the doors in, but he wasn't finished installing the windows, he woke to the sound of something banging around on the deck. He got up, grabbed a hatchet, and went to investigate. When he got to the kitchen, a black bear had stuck its head in one of the unfinished windows and he yelled at it. It roared back at him, a long melancholic honking sort of a roar he tried to imitate when he told the story. He was overwhelmed in that moment, not by fear, but by disgust at the stink of the thing, an eye-watering stink of rotting meat and garbage and human shit.

"It was the stink of civilization," her dad always said and then he would laugh. "And then it turned and ran off into the woods."

She tried to remember how he looked the first time he told her that story, but she could not, she could only put together her memories of her memories of him. She knew he was tall and lean, long-armed and whip-strong, a slight hook to his thin nose, clear blue eyes, receding red hair graying at the temples. She knew those things like he was a character in a book. She knew that was how he would have looked, should have looked, but she couldn't picture the incident of his telling the story itself. She was pretty sure he told it to her in the kitchen, in late summer, right after he came back from the cottage. They were sitting at the yellow Formica table, so it was before Mom had fixed up the kitchen, but she could not remember her father. She only knew he was there, at the table, telling her that story. His description of the bear was fixed in her mind; it was the story he repeated over and over again that seemed concrete, seemed real, not her father but his words.

Dave parked the van and their trailer across the road to block the path of digger semis with their loads of diesel. Then he made her stand between it and the oncoming trucks.

"Don't worry," he said. "They always stop, and when they do, they stand there until I get the hose hooked up. Once we're set up, the guy will wait until I'm finished. It's like milking a cow."

And the truck did roll to a gentle stop a few feet from Miranda, grill plastered with insects and the heat coming off it in waves. She looked up at the driver. It was a middle-aged woman, her grey hair pulled back in a ponytail. They stared at each other for a couple of seconds and then the driver looked out across the land.

Dave threw the van into gear and turned in a sharp arc to get himself parallel to the larger vehicle. It looked like a giant scurrying insect to Miranda, the van was a glittering head and thorax and the tank a fat abdomen. Dave pulled up tightly next to the semi and hopped out.

"You should be good now," he said. "They never take off once the process has begun."

He pulled on heavy gloves and was flipping switches in a control panel beneath the smooth curved belly of the tanker truck. Then he yanked open a cubby hole to the left of it and pulled out a big steel nozzle like a seahorse's head. He dragged it back to the van and clambered up to the top of his little tank, unscrewed the cap and slipped in the nozzle. He scrambled back and forth for a while: pulled out a pleated hose from a berth on the side of the truck, attached one end to one of a series of bent pipes that emerged from beneath the giant tank like a series of gills, tightened couplings, ran back to his trailer, attached the other end of the hose to the nozzle there, back to the truck, and re-examined everything there. The driver was still staring out across the fields. Another truck pulled up behind the first truck and was quietly parked.

"Alright," said Dave. "Here we go."

He opened a valve. He didn't leave it open for long before he shut it and ran back to the van's tank, scrabbled up, unscrewed the nozzle, and they were both hit by an acidic blast of diesel fumes.

"Alright," said Dave and reversed the whole process, carefully returning everything to where it had been, wiping things down with a rag, tightening and checking and double-checking.

"Let's go," he finally said and Miranda glanced up at the driver – still staring out across the fields.

There were five trucks lined up behind the one they stopped by the time they were on their way and they cruised past them slowly. None of the drivers bothered to look at them.

"How did you learn to do all that?" Miranda asked.

"Diggers," said Dave. "I looked at some old pamphlets and instruction books before I tried it, but it was them that taught me. I used to think I was robbing them, you know, used to think I was Robin Hood or something, would get a huge rush of euphoria, wave a handgun about at them, order them about and call them motherfuckers. But then, the first couple of times I did this, when they realized I didn't have a clue, they came down out of their cabs to help. Never a word or nothing. But I watched them enough that I figured it out on my own. Good teachers, diggers. Methodical."

"You don't think you're robbing them now?"

"Nope," said Dave. "I don't know what it is. I don't have a word for it, but it ain't robbing."

3

THEY CROSSED THE MISSISSIPPI well south of Minneapolis and then circled up to northwest of the city. The long, panoramic highways were swept clear of deserted vehicles, but there were fewer convoys, and while there were still plenty of diggings, they had seen no one working them since they reached the Great Plains. They barely talked. When Dave occasionally worked up the energy to get excited about something he saw or remembered or imagined, Miranda barely listened. His voice was part of a general soundscape to her: low rumbles, high-pitched exclamations, laughter, stops and starts, all blended seamlessly with the baritone growl of the engine, the thin hum of the tires on the asphalt, and the rush of the air around the car. Sometimes he would pause, perhaps to invite an interjection, perhaps to allow his thoughts to catch up to his words, and Miranda would be startled with the realization he was actually talking. On the whole, though, he had been relatively silent since Chicago. He would sit for long periods with his feet on the dashboard and stare out the windows.

The clear sky was smudged with a spattering of white and grey. The ditches along the highway were full of sparkling water and thick with cranes and ducks. The reedy banks fluttered with petulant songbirds. Many of the diggings here were old enough that they were covered with a dense growth of wild grasses and flowers. The ridges undulated in the wind, spasms rippling back and forth across the skin of the earth. There were also long, untouched stretches of deserted farmland, gravel and sand pits, galvanized steel sheds and storage facilities, massive concrete structures ribbed with tanks and scaffolding, isolated farmhouses and ancient, teetering barns, thin stands of spruce and pine marking the boundaries between properties, and sturdy, impenetrable windbreaks of tangled oak, ash and maple. Ragged cattle grazed in the weedy fields.

Miranda had driven these stretches of road all her life, first on local trips to visit family and friends, then longer journeys on vacations with her parents, and finally as a college student, making her way home across the great spans of the US for the summer, or heading back east in the fall, and what she saw now as she drove was as much her memory of the world she had constructed and reconstructed over the years as it was the world itself. It occurred to her that on those drives there had always been barriers between herself and the wind and the smells and the light of the prairie outside: the windows of the car, the tin doors, the muted violence of the engine's roar, the radio, the conversations, the long naps, and constant reading. She read hundreds of thousands of pages in the back seat as a kid and the passenger seat as an adult, millions of words consumed between innumerable glances out the window, and what she read and what she saw, only half-comprehendingly, in those introspective glances, had become as much a part of how she imagined herself and her life as any other part of her childhood and youth, but there was no real content to the experience, no coherence, there was no overriding narrative, no arc: it was all a purely arbitrary manufacture. It was as if the prairies had reached her as a disaggregation, a wave of discrete particles that had managed to slip through distorting fields of resistance, and which she had only subsequently organized into a pixelated whole.

The last book she could remember having read on such a trip was Dead Souls. She was bringing a roommate home for a visit, and she had been reading it out loud for them. The landscapes Gogol described seemed an echo of the landscape through which they were traveling. But now, so many years later, it was the landscape that seemed an echo of what she remembered of the book. Not the story, not the plot or the characters, but a few of the words – troika and census and serf; an intense anxiety about property rights; an evocation of what seemed a prairie spring. She remembered it was funny and satirical and sad, it was about open, expansive spaces, and a narrow, cramped society. She could not remember how the book ended, or how the trip ended, or even the fate of her relationship with that particular friend, all she knew for sure was what she felt then was somehow still there, in her experience of the blue sky and the distant horizon and the occasional stand of poplar and birch that gave the view depth and comprehensibility.

They ate lunch at a rest stop. They sat at a picnic table beside the parking lot eating cold beans out of cans. They looked out over an almost unbroken expanse of grass. Dave had been experiencing little seizures all morning. He said nothing, but twice Miranda watched him suffer from a sequence of jerking twitches, his legs and arms quivering, his lips smacking. He looked exhausted as they ate, washed out, almost grey. He was not taking care of himself as thoroughly as when they met. His hair was unkempt. There was sleep in his eyes and stains on his shirt.

"You OK, Dave?" she asked and he started.

"I'm fine," he said, "I'm fine."

When he finished his can of beans, he pushed it aside.

"Lost in a fog," he said. "Can't wake up."

Then he rose and went into the building.

Miranda closed her eyes. The sun warmed her; she could see it red through her lids, and the cool breeze blowing through the site was barely stimulation enough to keep her from nodding off. She heard the excited call of a meadowlark, a sliding, distorted warble that always reminded her of the sound of someone pressing fast-forward on an old-fashioned cassette player.

She opened her eyes and saw the bird sitting on a fencepost not ten feet away, a smear of yellow across the weathered grey of the wood. The meadowlark shouted at her once more and then was gone in a fluttering flash of wings. She put her head down on the worn out wood of the picnic table and closed her eyes. The breeze was no longer enough to keep her awake and when she opened her eyes again she was in a puddle of drool, with no idea how long she had been asleep. She looked around for Dave and didn't see him so she went into the rest stop building. It was a brown hexagon of painted plaster, glass, and timber. Dave was in the central hall between the two bathrooms staring at a map.

"Hey," Miranda said and he glanced at her.

"Hey."

She went into the women's toilet. It was in good condition. Two stalls, fold-down diaper table, pink soap in the dispenser. There was toilet paper on the rolls and a little drop box for needles. There was enough water to flush and some left in the taps as well. She washed her hands carefully, feeling the slick aggression of the industrial soap against her skin, enjoying its chemical smell, and then drying herself off on the linen towel for an inordinate length of time.

On the way out, she stopped to look at the map Dave was staring at earlier. Taped to the glass case was a typed pamphlet and the mimeograph of a hand drawn map:

"Join us at Big Echo Mine. We are a loving community always willing to welcome hardworking survivors into our fellowship."

The map was of western Montana and showed Big Echo as a black star. Miranda peeled it off, folded it neatly into a square, and slipped it into her pocket. Dave was waiting for her in the van when she emerged. The meadowlark was back on the post. She cleaned up their cans and wiped off the table.

It looked the same as every other community she passed through in the last few years. Deserted cars, broken windows in the storefronts, weeds growing in the cracks and potholes, crows on the wires. She barely even thought about where she was going, merely let the vehicle take her there: down Main

Street past the Presbyterian Church and left at the lights, follow the curve of the road into the ruined small town paradise of the gentle river valley. When she tried, she found she could remember the names of families who lived in the houses that crowded the pockmarked streets. She was briefly tempted to recite them for Dave: Larsons, Millers, Taylors, Schulzes. But it was real work to recollect anything concrete – faces, laughter, voices. It surprised her, this indifference of her memory to the stimulation of a homecoming. She had imagined an artesian gush. She worried about being overwhelmed by the return, but she felt no rush of sentimentality, no melancholy, no nostalgia, no grief. Just a sequence of indifferent thoughts, and behind them, the nausea of anticipation.

She parked in the driveway of her parents' modest bungalow, listening to the silence after the motor stopped. Dave was trying not to watch her too closely. He was pretending to look at the pamphlet and map she had taped to the windscreen.

"You want me to go in first?" he asked.

"No," she said. "I'll be fine."

"You want me to wait here or come with?"

"Wait here."

She got out of the van and walked up the steps. The door was unlocked and she walked in. Shafts of light cut through the air, illuminating a corner of the sofa, a patch of rug, a rhombus of pale paint on the wall. A soft veneer of dust lay on everything.

In the kitchen, the cat's water bowl and food dish were empty. She was startled to see a photo of herself on the fridge: her and Dad in the canoe, about to disembark, or maybe returning from a day trip. Dad was behind her, tanned and lean, eyes sparkling, the deep grooves of his smile carved out of his cheeks, paddle still in the lake, turning up a green swell of water. Miranda was in the front, looking up at the photographer: serious, sunburn splashed across her nose and cheeks. It was likely Mom took the picture, either relieved to see them return or relieved to see them go. There were some bills on the fridge as well. Some photos of children she couldn't remember, the children of cousins, maybe, second cousins, family friends.

The bedrooms upstairs were tidy. The queen in the master carefully made, jewelry on the vanity, a wedding photo, a brush with a bed of hair tangled between the tines, perfume – the usual Chanel, almost certainly an anniversary gift from her father. Miranda sprayed some on her wrist. Still no dizzying descent down the well of memory. She pulled open a drawer and saw the floral cover of a diary. She picked it up, running her hands over the textured satin, and then sat down with it on the bed. She opened it up on her lap but made no effort to read it, briefly touched the pages, followed the flow of the handwriting, the propulsive energy. She thought of Dave tearing the pages out of his notebooks and burning them in the hibachi. She returned it to its place with the scarves and gloves and went into the guestroom.

It was once her room but she had been gently erased from it during her years in college and New York. A sewing table and sewing machine replaced her desk and bookshelf. Overlapping swatches of fabric lay on the bed. A sunbeam fell across the fabric, the faded cotton showing the measured transitions of the light across the room. She was aware her mother used to sew, before her, before the career, but did not realize she had started again.

The cat was dead in the bathroom, beside the toilet where it would have smelled the water, an unmoving mat of fur and bone.

She went back through the kitchen to get to the dim garage and find the car. It was there. The workbench and tools. The old yellow table as well, tucked in the corner and piled with boxes. And the bikes: Dad's, Mom's, hers. Her kayak in the rafters. The lawnmower. She smelled oil, a hint of gas, wood, concrete. She opened the garage door and light flooded in. Dave was leaning against the van smoking a joint. He looked over and she shook her head.

They were on the road that would take them out of town, Miranda driving, Dave looking out the window.

"I thought there was going to be a "gone fishing" note on the table," she said. "The yellow one, the Formica one in the garage."

"Sorry, kiddo," said Dave.

"I'm sorry too," said Miranda. "But I can't quite decide why."

Dave let her sit in silence for a few blocks and then began to talk, more than he had talked in days. He had a new theory about things, about what happened, a theory about some kind of virus, about cat litter and mice feces and pregnant women. It had been percolating for some time and was a big theory. Miranda followed the gist of it for a while, and even made some objections to fuel the fire. It was nice to hear him talking again, thinking out loud, reacting. It was nice to listen to him as she drove, as they followed the road past the university buildings where her dad had taught, the classroom blocks and admin buildings, past the experimental fields and the greenhouse, past the car dealerships and the shopping mall and the riverside park now entirely overgrown, past the elementary school with orange buses parked outside, past the seed silos of the farmers' co-op and the fertilizer and chemical warehouse, past the big concrete grain silos along the tracks, past all the evidence of how things used to be, of how things were, of how they used to organize things in the ancient past, in the once upon a time. It was nice to hear Dave talk to her as they left it all behind.

4

"HOW BIG IS THAT VIEW?" asked Miranda.

They parked on a ridge overlooking an expanse of rolling grassland. The air saturated with sunlight.

"Gargantuan," said Dave and passed her the joint.

Miranda turned off the motor and took it.

"Bohee-a-mothic," Dave tried again.

She took a couple of puffs and blew a plume of smoke out the window.

"Hypermagnifico," she said and took a much longer pull.

"Superannihilationist," said Dave and Miranda coughed up the smoke with her laughter.

In the morning it was all spiky squalls of rain and Miranda had a headache. She couldn't convince Dave to wake up. When she got out of the van she stared up at the ridge for a while and then trudged up the road to its crest. She poked around up there, scuffed the dirt about with her boots, then continued down the other side. She followed the road for about a mile until she found some pronghorn watching her from across the ditch and went back for the gun.

There were three men standing beside the van. They had long hair and beards and carried hunting rifles. They were not diggers.

"Hi guys," she said, "what can we do for you?"

They said nothing. Miranda brushed by them and banged on the side panels.

"Dave," she shouted. "We have company!"

"How many of you are there?" asked one of the men.

"Just me and Dave."

"Where are you going?" asked the man.

"We heard there was a camp for regulars up in Montana," said Miranda and banged on the van again.

"Dave," she shouted. "For Chrissake, wake up!"

"How many people?" asked the man.

"What?" asked Miranda.

"How many people in this camp? How many regulars?"

"Wait a sec, guys," Miranda said. "I gotta check on my partner."

She walked to the back and yanked open the door. Dave was half out of his sleeping bag, eyes rolled up into his skull, skin grey.

"Shit," said Miranda and clambered in.

"Dave, wake up," she said and slapped his face.

He'd pissed himself and everything was cold and damp.

"Dave, come on," she said and he moaned.

The man stuck his head in.

"Epilepsy?" he asked.

"It's the whole fucking works," Miranda said, "seizures, schizoid episodes, weird twitches."

"And you?" asked the man.

"Miranda?" said Dave and she looked down into his frightened eyes. "Miranda?"

"It's OK, Dave, you were gone," she said. "But you came back."

"I'm sorry, Miranda," he said. "I'm sorry."

"Shut up, Dave," she said softly, and looked back at the man.

"What you say?" she asked the man.

"What's wrong with you?"

"I dunno," said Miranda. "Maybe brain cancer, some kind of tumor anyways, you tell me."

The man withdrew and Miranda pulled the .45 out of the glove compartment, tucked it into her belt and pulled her sweatshirt down over top.

"What's going on?" Dave was blinking up at her, eyes wide, voice thick.

Miranda shrugged.

"Who were you talking to?"

"Just some men, some guys passing through."

"Which guys?" Dave struggled into a reclining position and blinked out the window.

"Some guys that showed up out of nowhere," she said softly.

Dave sat up.

"Lie down," said Miranda, but Dave scrabbled out of his sleeping bag and grabbed the rifle. Then he clambered over to the back doors and sat there, dangling his legs over the edge, rifle across his knees. Miranda climbed past him.

The men were gone and Dave sat there peering about, looking threadbare and weak, exhausted.

"What men?" he asked. "Where?"

"Go lie down," said Miranda.

"It's not safe," said Dave.

"Go lie down," said Miranda.

"We have to get out of here, it's not safe."

"Fine. I can pack us up. You lie down."

"I'll help."

"Lie down."

"My gear is soaked. I have to wash it."

"Lay down on mine. I'll clean yours up. I'll do some other laundry too. I'll strap your sleeping bag to the tank when I've washed it, it can air out while we drive. It'll be springtime fresh tonight."

Dave wouldn't look at her.

"We don't have time for laundry," he said.

"Yes, we do," said Miranda. "Now go lie down."

When she came back from the stream with his sleeping bag Dave had retreated into the van. He was lying on his side on her bag with his hands between his knees staring at the paneling. She threw the bag on the tank, boiled some water, and made them some coffee. They drank it in silence, threw out the dregs, hitched up the trailer, and hit the road.

A few miles later they looked down from an escarpment and could see a whole sprawling works laid out below them. Massive, curving grooves cut out of the valley floor, curling and twisting into each other, sweeping up the side of the hills, stretching as far as the eye could see. Dozens of bulldozers, dump trucks, and land-movers crawled about the bottom of trenches, between the ribs, little yellow beetles picking a corpse clean.

Dave was huddled up on the passenger seat under a blanket, shivering, forehead pressed against the window.

"It's almost as big as the one we saw in South Dakota," he said.

"Maybe bigger," said Miranda.

"Remember the guy near Fargo who said he'd seen one in Texas?" Dave rubbed his eyes. "It stretched from horizon to horizon, in every direction, and no one working it, basically sitting there empty and waiting."

"Waiting for what?" He asked Miranda when she said nothing. "Waiting for what?"

Miranda put the van into gear.

"I didn't much like how those guys sounded," said Dave. "Those ones who confronted you."

"I wouldn't say 'confronted,'" Miranda said.

The highways were bare as bones in the desert, or in a city dump, bones worked over by the birds and the rats and the dogs.

"What you said about them reminded me of those assholes we met south of Cleveland," he continued. "You remember them? Those guys with the caravan?"

"Sure I do," said Miranda.

"Assholes," said Dave.

He closed his eyes, clenched his fists, and shouted: "Assholes!"

"I didn't much care for them either," said Miranda.

"Killers," said Dave and one of his hands twitched. "Killers."

They drove in silence for five minutes.

"I've been dreaming about those guys," said Miranda.

"The guys you just saw?"

"No, those three south of Cleveland."

"You've been dreaming about them?"

"Not all three. Not really. Just the one."

"Which one?"

"The one they called Smacksburg."

Dave laughed, "The little one?"

"I keep dreaming he's following us. That he followed us from their camp to Toledo, up to Chicago, Wisconsin, Minnesota, out west, the Dakotas, Wyoming, out here, up here onto the Great Plains. In my dreams I see him, on a motorbike, cutting across the landscape, scalpel sharp, cutting the country open, spilling out the coiled guts of it, trailing a strange kind of death in his wake, a kind of sterility, something dreadful."

Dave licked the joint shut and sparked it.

"I saw him this morning," said Miranda.

"Smacksburg?"

"Yeah."

"In your dreams?"

"No. I was awake. I saw him sitting on a dirt bike on the road where it ran over the ridge and he was looking down on us. A helmet on and a dog skull between the handlebars, but I knew it was him. I knew it. Real as real. Then he turned around and took off. I walked up there and looked around: no tracks, no dust in the air, no smell of gas, no sign of him. I kept walking and walking but there were no signs. No signs. Then I found some pronghorn and came back for the gun and those other fellows had shown up while I was gone."

"That's fucked up," said Dave and passed her the joint.

"I know," said Miranda.

"You're a mess," said Dave. "Getting haunted by a no-account pissant like that when you got so many mad bastards to choose from."

Miranda gave him the doobie back.

"Even his buddies," said Dave. "Even his buddies make more sense. That Rasputin guy with the eyes like radio telescopes, shooting x-rays out of his skull, counting your fillings, counting your bones. Or the blond beast daydreaming about feasting on our subaltern livers, I could see being haunted by those sonsofbitches, but Smacksburg? Gettng haunted by Smacksburg is like getting haunted by homeless Steve Buscemi."

Miranda's vision inspired Dave to start spinning stories about what he called their post-apocalyptic situation. He didn't call them stories. He would wink at Miranda when she called them lies. Dave preferred the term proofs, because he imagined himself in an argument with Miranda about how radical the break between the present and the past was. It was an impressive catalogue of human types he invented and he would run through it while Miranda drove, while he cooked them their suppers, while they shared a drink and a toke in the evening:

skulls on stakes and Caucasian dudes with beards cutting themselves up with razor blades before they went to war with each other; terrorists and prophets and troubadours; refugee encampments and convoys of cheerful daydreaming enthusiasts driving up to Canada-the-great-white-hope where they said there was still electricity, plumbing, vaccinations, pension plans, universities, and science, so much science, science growing in the fields and raining from the skies, an endless harvest of science; little clusters of true-believing pessimists killing time until the big finish; deliberate junkies methodically looting the pharmacies and the hospitals; angry patriotic dads with assault rifles and RVs and water-purifying systems trying to keep their depressed pill-popping wives and illiterate pyromaniac children in line with Bible verses and ritual promises and the constant, rumbling, subliminal threat of their suicide-murder Abraham-begat-Isaac prayer-noise; bandit chuffers; survival-heads; hippie dirtbags; glory singers; Nazi baby farmers; zucchini planters; murder Christians; might-as-well-be Christians; love Christians; happy Christians; suburban-get-alongers; philosophical nihilists; practical nihilists; schmihilist nihilists; dog walkers; nature zealots; sewer troglodytes; hospital zombies; Color Purple homesteaders; weed people; poppy people; meth people; shazbots; scarecrows; acid splashers; good cannibals; bad cannibals; cannibal cannibals; and on and on and on he went populating the whole empty span of his imaginary post-America.

And she remained unconvinced, so one day while he was stewing some rhubarb he harvested from the corner of a farmhouse, he told her about these guys called the White Wolves: bikers from the south, from Louisiana, from East Texas, who came up north every summer, looting the petty bourgeois settlements and condominium fortresses and the gated Jerusalems alike: with long beards, eyes like weeping sores, yellow teeth. They burned it all down. Like what happened in Cleveland. With those assholes. With those Nazi assholes in Cleveland. They burned the few remaining stands of civility and decorum down to the ground. In the winter they would head south into Mexico, and in the summer come ranging up the Mississippi, up over the Appalachians, to cut the ears off people for their Mardi Gras necklaces and fly bloody scalps from aerials on the back of their bikes. He met this guy they had attacked; they ran him off the road, shattered his window and reached in to get at his ears and his hair. Then they left him strapped into the car and roared away. When he healed up the guy looked like a peeled grapefruit.

"Like a peeled grapefruit!" Dave repeated.

In Indiana he came across a Kumbayah camp they raided, mostly just bits and pieces left, but a couple of mangled women still alive.

"Moaning," Dave said. "Moaning."

He told her these stories and more, so many more, but she was bored. She felt like she had heard them all before. She was drinking a Château Potensac, which Dave found in an unexpected small town wine store and insisted was top-shelf big city swill. She drank it straight from the bottle and finished a joint while she stared out across the empty fields of weeds and saplings where wheat and canola and flax once grew. All she could think of while he tried to horrify her was how good a crumble would be on that rhubarb, and some ice cream, but when Dave finally paused and stared at her, eyebrows raised as they were whenever he felt he'd won an argument, or at least scored some points, she felt like she should respond.

"There is nothing post-apocalyptic about violent men getting what they want, Dave," she said.

They didn't stop in Billings. Dave didn't like driving through the empty cities and towns. He kept reminding her that the buildings looked like gravestones, and the gravestones reminded him of his kids. So they didn't stop in Billings. Instead, they found a cluster of deserted fast food joints, gas stations, and liquor stores on the outskirts and stopped there. The skyline shone copper in the setting sun as they got drunk.

"I'm feeling inexpressibly, unaccountably happy," said Dave. He was roasting a hot dog over the fire. He had found a can of them in a gas station.

"You shouldn't be eating those dogs," said Miranda.

"I'm feeling jubilant, ecstatic, delighted," said Dave. "And that's never good."

"Really? It sounds pretty good."

"It's not. It is not good. A big electrical storm is brewing somewhere in my brainstem. I always get these excited, tingling jolts of euphoria before a big explosion."

"Maybe it's the Jim Beam and flat Coke," said Miranda.

"Maybe," said Dave.

Later, he set off hundreds of dollars' worth of corner store fireworks.

He pretended a roman candle was his pecker and chased Miranda about the parking lot with it, spraying molten gold and silver into the darkness. When he opened another bottle of bourbon, Miranda went to bed. In the early hours of the morning, he crawled into the van and curled up beside her.

"You're alright, kiddo," he whispered and when she didn't respond he shook her awake.

"What the hell, Dave," she said,

"I wanted to let you know, you're alright," he whispered.

"Why are you whispering?"

"I wanted to let you know, you're alright," he continued whispering. "And I love you."

"I love you too, you fucking idiot, now let me sleep."

Dave spent most of the next day puking so they stayed. The day after that it poured rain and Miranda didn't feel like driving so Dave sat in the van and picked over Miranda's books before he settled on Sleepless Nights by Elizabeth Hardwick and curled up in the passenger seat. Miranda dozed for most of the morning, but by early afternoon she was bored. She pulled on a poncho and some rubber boots and went for a walk.

The rain was falling so hard the poncho was plastered to

her head and shoulders and the water battered the plastic into eerily topographic patterns. The drainage ditches were filled with twisting floods of brown water that looked thick as syrup. Miranda stepped into one and stumbled against the current, the rubber boots flattening against her. It felt like a pair of strong hands seizing her feet and ankles. She had a flashback to early childhood: standing in a deep, sparkling puddle after a storm, feeling the weight of it compressing her boots, sliding one foot forward until the water spilled over the rim of the boot in a smooth, contoured vortex, shuddering at the cold as it filled her boot and equalized the pressure.

On the other side of the ditch, through the falling sheets of rain, Miranda could make out the ghostly, squat shape of a box store. She trudged across the flooded parking lot. It was a grocery store and she stepped inside, into gloom, and began to explore. It was unlooted. She went first, from habit, to the pharmaceuticals and admired the carefully ordered boxes and bottles in their rows; pristine, virgin objects in a lost tomb. She pocketed some ibuprofen and then found the Maxi-pads and the tampons. She wandered through the toiletries, testing the lotions on the back of her hand, smelling the soaps, examining the labels of the shampoos and the conditioners as if she were shopping. She briefly considered stripping naked and washing herself in the parking lot, lathering up her hair into slippery ropes and letting the storm wash the suds away, but the thought of the cold made her shiver and she felt an unaccountable thrill of modesty at the thought of all the open space beyond the curtains of the rain. Besides, by the time she stacked some supplies by the front door for later collection it looked like it was easing up. She went back into the aisles and dug up some tinned anchovies and olives and a case of Pellegrino to surprise Dave and carried them past the checkout.

The storm had blown through but it was to be a brief respite. Shafts of soft light were drifting with the showers and the mist across the glittering parking lot, but another bank of clouds was illuminated to the west: a shifting wall of greys and whites, the tops of the clouds glowing brightly in the heat of the sun, the bottoms a dark smudge of disintegration. It was sweeping slowly towards them. A long row of transmission towers, aluminum latticework shining, marched off towards the coming onslaught. They looked to Miranda like rock paintings of not-quite human figures, stiff-backed abstractions, meditations on gods who could no more survive the relentless press of chaos and disorder than could humanity. The nearest of the structures towered above Miranda, powerlines still clutched tightly in their claws, colossi watching over the cluster of buildings that grew up around this intersection of trade routes. So huge when they rose directly above you, they were diminished as they approached the horizon, dwindling away until they were swallowed up by the looming clouds.

5

THEY RAN OUT OF GAS IN THE FOOTHILLS and decided to hike the rest of the way.

"I sure hope someone's still there," said Dave. He peeled the pamphlet off the window and jammed it into his pocket.

"If anyone ever was," said Miranda and locked the door.

"Why you doing that?" asked Dave. "We're not coming back. Leave it open, with the keys in the ignition. If someone finds it, they can have it."

"I guess it's stolen anyways."

"Not stolen; appropriated," Dave looked up into the mountains, "by the Holy Remnant Liberation Front and Repopulation Society."

"Repopulation?" Miranda laughed. "I think you got the wrong idea about the nature of the state of our relationship, Dave."

"It's not about us, baby," said Dave. "It's about humanity. It's about the future. You think there's cougars up there?"

"Oh yeah," said Miranda, "looking at us right now, licking their chops at the thought of appropriating your swollen greasy liver."

"Cougars don't appropriate," said Dave. "They just take."

He shivered, "Take, take, take."

"Bastards," he whispered. "Bastards."

They followed an old highway north through the forested hills. The tarmac was cracked and withered, grass and rubble were starting to break it up. It was a splitting seam, but they figured it must have seen occasional use since things changed. There was evidence of foot traffic – old fires, discarded clothes, tin cans, plastic bottles. It was high summer and hot, which meant Dave tired frequently and had to stop, but fresh water wasn't a problem and there were plenty of old lodges and camp-grounds about, places where they could get some rest and grub about for canned goods.

"Eventually," said Dave as they waited for the creamed corn to heat up in the embers of some tourist trap's parking lot fire pit, "we're going to get botulism and die. That's how it'll all end for our species, hundreds of thousands of years of evolution: language, culture, science, industry. The last human will expire in a flood of shit and vomit, colonized by bacteria painstakingly sealed into a tin can for safekeeping by some underpaid worker a half century earlier."

"I've got some rice if the corn makes you nervous," said Miranda. "And lentils, although it'll take a bit."

"Yeah, well," said Dave. "I'm hungry now."

They were camped beside a bend in a river that ran along the highway. The sun was setting behind them and they were watching the shadow creep slowly up the forested slopes on the other side.

"The Nez Perce came up through here, you know," Dave said. "Or through some place like it. You know the story of the Nez Perce?"

Miranda shook her head.

"I had this prof, way back when, a thousand years ago or more, when I was young, when the world was young, but this story was already old when he told it to us," Dave lapsed into recollection.

"It was after the Battle of Little Bighorn, after Custer was killed and Sitting Bull fled north," he said. "The Nez Perce were next on the US government shit list I guess, all those white people hungry for land and not caring too much about how the government acquired it, so the US Army bravely chased them up out of Idaho and Oregon into these parts. They fought this running battle, that's how I remember the prof telling it, up through Montana towards the Canadian border where they thought they could find refuge, like Sitting Bull."

Dave paused to think about it.

"It's funny I'm starting so very close to what people generally consider to be the end of the story," he said. "But it's not. It's not the end at all."

There was a long pause before he continued.

"So," he said. "Anyways. This old professor of mine always told this story, gave this lecture, full of detail and names and color, last day of his western US history course, and he always ended the class with the speech the chief gave when they were caught. A set piece. Chief Joseph. I don't know his real name anymore. The chief's name. I forgot it. But anyways. He cried whenever he performed it. The professor, not the chief. I asked him about it later and he said he cried every year, every time he gave it, tears streaming down his cheeks. Even though he suspected the whole thing was a fake, a translator's forgery. It didn't matter. He always cried. The whole class was rapt, enthralled; it was peak Dead Poets Society shit. And I was so blown away I memorized it. I memorized it."

Dave stood up. The hills were almost entirely lost to gloom now, the long shadows of the mountains swallowing them up, only the very rim of them currently golden, the cutting edge gleaming. Miranda sat up on an elbow to watch Dave. He straightened his back, head up, twitched a couple of times and began:

"I am tired of fighting. Our chiefs are killed. Looking Glass is dead. Toohoolhoolzoote is dead. The old men are all dead. It is the young men who say, 'Yes' or 'No.' He who led the young men is dead. It is cold, and we have no blankets. The little children are freezing to death. My people, some of them, have run away to the hills, and have no blankets, no food. No one knows where they are – perhaps freezing to death. I want to have time to look for my children, and see how many of them I can find. Maybe I shall find them among the dead. Hear me, my chiefs! I am tired. My heart is sick and sad. From where the sun now stands I will fight no more forever."

Dave's voice broke on "forever" and he stopped, eyes welling, and looked away. Off into the hills. He sighed.

"'I will fight no more forever,'" Dave said. "That's exactly the same spot it was for the professor. Same word: forever. That's exactly the same place in the speech where the White Guilt would hit him and the bourgeois motherfucker would begin to weep."

Dave talked the whole of the following day. He told Miranda stories about mountain men and jamborees and prospectors he learned about as a schoolboy and in college. He told her stories from books he'd read as an adult, stories about Manifest Destiny and the 49th and the 54th parallels and bloody meridians and filibusters and the lying, murdering bastards whom the lying, cowardly bastards who wrote history books liked to call statesmen. He told her new stories he'd heard from strangers around campfires, stories heard while men passed liquor back and forth, stories told while food and drugs were shared and exchanged, stories about troglodytes growing mushrooms and farming rats in the sewers, salvage capitalists trying to bully deserted factories back into life for imaginary markets, he told her stories about what he called the "sea cracker fleets," poor white folk on the Gulf Coast and around Florida, living on barges in the rising flood. He told her stories he'd imagined and dreamed, in convulsive bursts of words, fairy tales about valleys filled with human bones, and fabulous gardens growing in the white ash soil of the moon, and the quiet children who watched them from the waiting woods, and how the wind whistled "Ode to Joy" as it blew across the flues of the chimney stacks at the Mitchell Power Plant in Moundsville, West Virginia.

And the whole time, Miranda only interrupted him twice: once to point out a bear on the other side of the river, an interruption that shut him up for a half hour or so, and the second time to ask for the pamphlet and map from his pocket, so they could decide when they needed to leave the highway and start cutting through the bush towards the mountain where the camp was supposed to be.

Dave shrugged his shoulders when she asked his opinion and started talking about how much easier it would be if they had a helicopter.

"My buddy used to take me up in his, on the East Coast," said Dave. "We called him the Conductor because he was epileptic and every time he took you up you wondered if this was the day when he would stamp your ticket."

"I thought you called him Roulette," said Miranda.

"We called him lots of things," said Dave. "Have you ever seen the diggings from the air?"

"Nope," said Miranda.

"Fantastic," said Dave. "Phantasmagoric, even. Hallucinatory. Always put me in the mind of indecipherable ancient scripts, fluid-looking from up top, dynamic. I used to squint at them, imagine them as pictographs, like those gigantic ones in Chile or Peru that are meaningless at ground level and only make sense from the sky, but these weren't simple figures, of course, no stick men but absurdly complex, so much more complicated. I used to look for repetition, patterns, discrete shapes emerging from the chaos, some sign of order in them. Sometimes they looked like something you'd see under a microscope, you know? In a slide. All mitochondrial, all viral, all incomprehensible design, all unknowable, alien intelligence."

"Let's keep heading north," said Miranda. "We'll cross the river at the next bridge."

They were watching the sunrise through a gap in hills, an acid wash more than a ball of fire. Miranda was making coffee. The pot, settled into the embers of the previous night's fire, was coming to a boil.

"It's always a first sunrise, isn't it?" Dave said. "You can never remember the ones you've seen before."

He waited for Miranda to say something but she was too intent on her task.

"You think you can remember them, but you can't," Dave continued. "You only have an idea you remember them. You can't remember actual, specific sunrises, can you? You can't remember the actual event, it's always just a synthesis of all the many sunrises you've seen over the course of a lifetime. You have an idea of what a sunrise is, a pretty accurate idea, sure, but not a memory of the thing itself."

Miranda removed the pot from the fire and put it on a rock.

"It's like those crazy fuckers who used to make composite photographs of criminals, you know?" said Dave. "In the nineteenth century. Lombroso and Galton and all those other dead Darwinians. Hundreds and hundreds of photos merging to create an image of the ideal criminal."

"Average," said Miranda.

"What?"

"Not ideal," said Miranda. "Average."

"Really?"

"I think so," said Miranda and stirred coffee into the water, watching it darken, thicken, turn to oil. "Yeah."

"Does it matter?"

"No," said Miranda. "Not really."

"So anyways," says Dave. "What you remember when you think you remember a sunrise is only the composite of a lot of mostly forgotten sunrises, all the empty gaps and blank spots filled in by your imagination, not an actual, historical sunrise that really happened, simply the idea of a sunrise."

Dave kept talking as Miranda watched the eastern sky. One

morning, when she was home from college in the summer, she had partied with her old high school friends at her Dad's cottage. They were all passed out on couches, in sleeping bags in cars, and on pillows on the floor. Everyone except her and this one boy she hadn't met before, someone's cousin, she couldn't remember his name but he came from a city and had never been to lake country before: never seen the massive rocks looming up like stone idols from the dark waters, stained with lichen and moss, crowned with fir and pine trees, never heard the rush of wind in the poplars, the loons, the lapping of the water on the shore. This kid was nineteen or twenty and was so awestruck by it all he hadn't gone to sleep with the rest of them after the beer ran out, but just sat there on the deck staring out at the glassy water as the sky lightened, excited to see this new world again. Miranda took him down to the dock, and threw a life jacket on him, grabbed a rod-and-reel, put him in the canoe, and paddled him out to the middle of lake. She sat back and watched the arc of his throws, enjoying the ratcheting whizz, the plop of the sinker, his silent excitement at the raw, fresh experience of it all. It was a clear, bone-grey sky and coils of mist lingered in the coves and bays, there were no bugs out, the woods were now lost in undifferentiated shadow and were beginning to wake up, to come alive with birds and the beginnings of a breeze. The sun did not so much rise above the scene, over the dark serration of the treetops, as it formed there, a growing intensity of a light, a concentration of heat and energy drawn up from the world around it, a sort of a vortex. Unbelievably, this kid from the city caught a fish, a small jack; Miranda unhooked it for him and let him hold it before she released it, feeling the twist of its muscles, a slick undulation as it darted away into the thick, cool water, a mottled flash vanishing into the darkness.

Dave was still talking when she splashed some cold water into the coffee, waited a few seconds for it to settle the grounds, and carefully filled their tin cups with the black, syrupy brew.

That afternoon they were following an overgrown logging road through some scrawny larch and pine. Dave was walking a few feet ahead of Miranda when he keeled over, face smashing into the dry mud. He quivered and twitched in the rutted track. Miranda dropped her backpack and ran to him. She rolled him over to see the whites of his eyes like boiled eggs and blood frothing through his clenched teeth. She didn't know what to do so she lay down with him, holding him tight, pressing his head against her chest, feeling the strange energy surging up and down his thin body, smelling the piss and the sweat, listening to him moan.

Miranda set up camp at the edge of some old clearcut; she found a patch of sheltered meadow beside a stream. Dave twisted his ankle when he fell and it was swollen and purple, the tissue straining at the taut skin.

"You're going to have to go ahead," said Dave while he rolled his joint.

"Maybe," said Miranda.

"Not maybe," said Dave. "I can't walk. You can't carry me. You have to find some help."

"I wasn't kidding about the cougars up here," said Miranda.

"So leave the gun," said Dave and licked the joint shut. "Not that I'd be such a great loss to humanity."

"I don't give a fuck about humanity," said Miranda. "Fuck humanity."

"Second order abstractions," said Dave and lit up: "always the first thing out the window when the shit hits the fan."

Miranda refused to leave until she spent the rest of the day and the night with him. He was in agony and couldn't sleep. In the morning the ankle looked worse. He said his toes were tingling, so she let him talk her into trying to find the people on her own and send help. She walked the rest of the day and well into the night. There was no moon and the forests closed in, leaving only a narrow trail of stars visible directly above her. She struggled along in the dark until she started to trip over her feet from the weariness. She built a little fire by the side of the road, heated up some water for tea and pulled a blanket tightly around her shoulders. She had left all the food with Dave and was hungry.

She woke up in the middle of the night with her heart pounding, cold sweat on her back and forehead, freezing, the fire out, the stars behind clouds, the world void. In a panic she scrabbled together some twigs and tinder and after a few trembling, sparkling strikes of the flint got the whisper of a flame to manifest. She fed it more kindling and breathed on it gently until it twisted and turned and began to grow, dancing. Then more kindling, more twigs, some shards of sweet-smelling larch, and there was a circle of light again.

Miranda relaxed, rubbed her eyes, stared into the darkness, puzzled at how it seemed less cold now, less empty. The malevolence that had woken her dissipated, the sense of a weird intelligence watching her, the old childhood fears that keep one motionless in bed, unable to move, unable to open one's eyes, that spirit was driven away by the burst of her activity, by the fragile light and meagre warmth of the fire.

V

THE GRAVE

1

THE NEXT TIME SHE OPENED HER EYES the sun was up and she was not alone. Two kids were staring at her. One of them was pointing a shotgun at her with alarming unsteadiness. The other had prodded her awake with his foot and jumped back. They were twelve or thirteen years old at most, in blue jeans and flannel shirts.

"It's OK," she said. "I'm a friend."

"Sure you are," said the one with the gun.

"I need your help," said Miranda. "My buddy has a broken ankle."

"We gotta take her back to base, Mitch," said the kid who woke her.

"I told you," said Miranda, "my buddy needs help. I don't have time for this bullshit. We need to go help him."

"We gotta take her back," the kid said.

"Up you get," said Mitch. "We have to check in before we do anything."

"But he could die."

"Up."

Miranda considered them. Mitch looked frightened but resolute: the gun more steady now, lips drawn tight, jaw firm. The other was scared, eyes wide, quick shallow breaths, jumpy, more manageable, more malleable. But Mitch was the one with the gun.

They walked for an hour, Miranda impatiently trying to pick up the pace and the boys unconcerned, before they finally emerged from the trees. The land was rolling and open, falling away towards the east. The road led them around a rise and skirted the precipice of an old strip mine. The massive stepped ledges were a desert of weeds and sage. Machines sat abandoned at the bottom of a titanic crater, their colossal limbs fixed in mid-reach. A gravel road brought them around the great hole and up through the hills to a fenced administrative compound: a couple of corrugated steel Quonset huts and a prefabricated office block. A tall, thin man with ragged hair like dreadlocks stood at the gate watching them.

"Hey Pete," said Mitch. "How you doing?"

Pete stared at Miranda as they walked past.

"Not talking today, Pete?" asked Mitch, without looking back.

A few people came out of the metal sheds as they approached the main building; women in sober dresses with their hair tucked under handkerchiefs, kids clustered around them. Miranda could smell livestock and heard the rumbling of a generator. Mitch banged on the door.

"Come on in!" someone shouted.

The room was filled with food supplies and power tools. A man stood at a desk poking around in the guts of a chainsaw. He wore a dirty ball cap with a sharply curved brim, a plaid shirt tucked into oil-stained jeans, and work boots.

"Well hullo," he said. "Who's this?"

"Hey, Dad," said Mitch. "We found her camping up near Brokenhead Creek."

"Did you now? And what were you doing up there?"

"Hunting. We were hunting."

"Hunting what? Up at Brokenhead?"

"She says she's got a hurt friend out there past the clearcut," said Mitch.

"Man or woman?" asked the man.

"What's the difference?" asked Miranda.

"Man," said Mitch.

"How bad's he hurt?" asked the man.

"Broken ankle," said Miranda.

"You and Ralph take the four-wheelers, grab Doc Smitty, and go fetch this guy," said the man and looked at Miranda. "Tell him you're friends of, what's your name, young lady?"

"Miranda."

"Tell him you're friends of Miranda."

"I'd just as soon go along," said Miranda.

"No room," said the man.

"I want to go along," she said.

"No," said the man and turned to the boys. "Now git."

The boys left and the man stepped out from behind the desk.

"Albert Renus," he said, wiped his hands off on his jeans and stuck out a big, calloused paw. "Wonderful to meet you, Miranda, and welcome to Big Echo."

It occurred to Miranda if she simply powered through the night and kept walking, Dave would have already been found and picked up.

Albert led her outside. It was still early in the morning and slightly overcast. Everything was suffused with a soft light and the air was perfectly still.

"We haven't had anyone new show up here for quite a while," he said. "Not since last summer. Almost a year."

"Everyone is dying," said Miranda. "They are giving up."

"Perhaps they are," said Albert. "Out there, at any rate, out in the world."

He lifted up his hat and scratched his scalp.

"So where are you, and, um..."

"Dave," said Miranda.

"Where are you and Dave coming from?"

"Out east," she said.

Albert chuckled.

"That's pretty vague," he said.

Miranda shrugged.

"We were just wandering about, I guess," she said. "We met in what used to be Pennsylvania and sort of drifted west together."

"Drifted," said Albert, "that's an evocative word, isn't it? A dangerous word."

"I suppose it depends," said Miranda.

"It does?" asked Albert. "On what?"

"On what sort of associations it has for you."

"Well," Albert frowned. "Rootlessness, right? People floating whichever way the wind blows them, no order to their lives, no meaning, a lack of willpower. That's what it means to me: someone who rejects the idea of purpose and duty. To me, someone who drifts is someone who rejects obligation and authority. Someone who follows the laziest sorts of personal inclinations with no thought to the future. The sort of person who thinks it is wonderful to be blown about whichever way by the wind, like dandelion down, someone lying on the bottom of a boat staring at the clouds in the sky, not thinking on where the current is taking them. People who drift, who don't make choices, abscond from their moral responsibility and inevitably end badly, surrounded by bad people, in bad places. That's what it evokes for me: a poorly lived life and a lonely death."

Albert waited for Miranda to respond but she did not.

"How did you hear about us?" asked Albert.

Miranda shrugged again.

"Was it one of our flyers?'

A young woman named Sarah took Miranda to a collection of picnic tables in what had once been a massive maintenance shed. Some women worked at a bank of old electric ovens at the far end, their laughter bouncing off the metal walls.

"Sit," said Sarah and went to talk to the women. She came back with a bowl of tomato soup and some cornbread. She sat opposite Miranda and watched her eat.

"I heard you have a friend coming."

"Dave," said Miranda.

"Is he OK?"

"He broke his ankle, but he should be alright."

"Good," said Sarah. "There are so few men here; Albert and the Doctor and Peter and the boys. And Peter's getting worse."

"What do you need men for?" asked Miranda.

"For hunting and machinery and stuff."

"Stuff, eh?" said Miranda. "Dave's alright. He's a mess, of course, seizures and whatnot, but he can function, he can manage 'stuff.'"

"How's the soup?" asked Sarah.

"Fantastic," said Miranda. "The soup is divine. Exquisite."

Sarah showed her to the single women's bunks.

"You can sleep here if your friend doesn't get here tonight, or if he arrives late, then they'll figure out alternative arrangements. We haven't had any couples in a while."

"His name is Dave," said Miranda. "And we're not a couple."

"Dave," said Sarah. "How long have you been traveling together?"

"Since this summer."

"I sometimes miss it," said Sarah. "Being on the road, moving from place to place, but I got so tired and lonely. Big Echo is a blessing. It's nice to have someone to share the work with. And the worry. It's the hardest part I think, about the road, all the worrying and wondering and thinking about what next? What next?"

"You don't worry about 'what next' here?"

"Not really," said Sarah. "Not in the same way. Here, with the others, you feel like you can make a mistake or two without it all ending in catastrophe. Here, you always have someone who will help you get out of the trouble you make for yourself. More people means more help, more help means less worry, less worry means more time for joy."

"Joy?" said Miranda, "Whenever I see a lot of people I just

see a lot of relationships to navigate and start to feel exhausted."

"You've been ruined for society," laughed Sarah. "You've gone wild."

"Have I? Well, Dave hasn't. Dave likes to have people around. At least he thinks he does. And that's what matters, right? What you think you like."

"Well, I think you'll like it here," said Sarah. "And I think we'll like having you. You and Dave. That's what I think."

They watched the kids playing outside: blond, nut-brown animals, teeth flashing in laughter.

"Are any of them yours?" asked Miranda.

"Jesse," she said and the smallest of them stopped his play to stare at them.

"Is his Dad gone out to the diggings?"

"No," said Sarah. "Jesse was born after it all happened, after the visitation, he was born here. Albert's his father."

"Visitation? That's a fancy name for it."

"It's Albert's word."

They heard the buzz of the four-wheelers. A second later they came chugging up the road from the mine. Mitch was on the first one, Ralph immediately after, with a white haired old man on the seat behind him.

"Where's Dave?" Miranda heard herself say. "Where's Dave? They don't have Dave."

2

BY THE TIME MIRANDA GOT TO THE administration building Mitch was talking to his father, the old man standing to one side.

"Something got to him, he was already in pieces. We gathered up all the bits we could find and buried them."

Miranda cleared her throat and Mitch looked at her.

"Sorry," he said and walked over to his four-wheeler. He

grabbed Dave's rucksack and the rifle from the back.

"Here," he said. "I think we got everything, but if you want I can take you out there tomorrow."

"Thanks," said Miranda. "I'd appreciate it."

"There's no need to go back." It was the old man; he must have been in his seventies, bent at the shoulders, head thrust forward, blue eyes watering.

"We searched the area pretty good," he said and stuck out a shaking hand. "John Smith, but everybody calls me Doc Smitty."

"I'm Miranda." She put down the bag and shook his hand, it felt light and dry as a feather.

"Sorry about your friend," said Doc Smitty.

"Me too," said Miranda. She pulled the bolt back on the rifle and a shell casing popped out of the chamber.

They left her alone in the office. She sat at Albert's desk. The chainsaw was still in bits and pieces and she could smell the oil. It was easy enough to make sense out of most of it, out of the big pieces at least, although the small ones were a bit of a mystery. The steel blade emblazoned with the word Husqvarna, the chain in its lumpy coils, and the bright orange shell were all straightforward. Miranda picked up the sparkplug and measured its heft in her palm. But the bolts and washers scattered about were meaningless to her, strange gears with raised teeth, flat stainless steel plates, clear tubes, cords, filters, and molded plastic bric-a-brac. She put her head down on the desk. She could see herself there in her mind's eye, as if she was watching from the door: long arms folded into a cushion, the curve of her back, greasy hair pulled back into a ponytail, her neck dirty, eyes blank.

"Poor Dave," she said out loud and her voice sounded to her like it was someone else talking. She felt sick. "Poor Dave, all alone in the woods. Poor Dave."

She kept saying it, over and over again, and the more she said it the sicker she felt: "Poor Dave."

"Poor Dave."

"Poor Dave."

"Poor Dave."

But no matter how many times she said it, the words didn't sound like hers. It sounded like someone else, but who? But who? Whose words were these? And for whom was she performing?

She imagined Dave shaking his head at her:

"Disassociation," she imagined him saying: "Dissociation, alienation, abjuration."

In the morning she woke up to find someone had cleared the chainsaw parts away and thrown a blanket over her shoulders.

Doc Smitty eventually appeared with a cup of instant coffee and showed Miranda around the compound. The tour ended with them standing next to a mound of coal at least forty feet tall.

"We burn it all winter," said the Doctor. "So we know it won't be hypothermia that finishes us off. And we got sheep, chickens, a few pigs, and there's cattle wandering around out there too, so we won't starve."

"What'll it be, then, that does finish you off?"

"Finish us off? It'll be heart failure for me. For the others it'll be massive seizures, malignant tumors, lots of suicide. The kids? Who knows? Most of them will join all the others, out there on the high plains, digging their holes."

"Joining the diggers, it's not quite the same, is it?" said Miranda, "As being finished off."

"Most people around here think it's a lot worse," said Doc Smitty.

Albert sat at the head of the table and said grace. Miranda stared at all the bent heads and calm faces, when her gaze fell on Albert. He was staring back at her.

"And when it is ours to pass from time to eternity," his blue eyes were pushed deep into their sockets, "own us and crown us heirs to thy kingdom. These favors and blessings we ask in the name of Christ, our Great Redeemer, amen."

The shuffle of chairs and the clatter of cutlery broke their gaze.

"So are there still those, Miranda," Albert's voice cut through the murmur of conversation, "who believe this visitation is not the punishment of God?"

"You mean out there, in the world?" She spooned some boiled potatoes onto her plate. "Or are you really only asking about me?"

"Both," said Albert.

"Most of the folks I met figured some sort of alien intelligence came down from outer space and possessed everyone." She passed the potatoes to Ralph.

Albert snorted.

"Government mind control experiment gone wrong is always popular, mass hysteria too. A few optimists are still arguing it's evolution. Dave was convinced it was viral. He decided that anyways. Pretty recently. He'd narrowed it down to a mutation in either the Epstein-Barr or the virus pregnant women get from cat litter."

"And you?"

"Me? I think people talk a lot of shit. Pass the butter, please."

They prayed and sang together every morning, every evening, and before meals. Albert read Bible verses to them, and talked a lot of cheerful banalities about social harmony. There were a dozen more-or-less functional adults and teenagers, the same number of kids, and about twice as many people in need of constant care in the shed they called the hospital. There was a big vegetable garden at the bottom of the hill, clothes to be cleaned and mended, meals to be cooked, children to be taught, so there was plenty for the women to do. The seven women and Miranda slept together at the back of one of the big steel sheds. Albert and Doc Smitty and the boys had cots in the admin building. Tall, ragged Pete came and went, never speaking unless he was spoken to.

And there were services, endless service, both planned and spontaneous, with the usual singing and praying and sermons and essays and assorted discourse on the importance of spiritual hygiene, mental cleanliness, purity of thought and conduct. The children especially were prayed over and blessed and celebrated. Sometimes these ceremonies broke down into a chaos of hosannas and hallelujahs and the names of saints and angels were evoked along with Father, Son and Holy Ghost. People would fall into each other's arms, twitching and foaming. Eyes would roll. There would be weeping and laughter, guttural barks, slurred vowels and staccato consonants, endless incomprehensible shouts.

In the center of the storm was Albert, always Albert, a Jupiter with his many staggered and various moons in orbit, his gravity holding them in thrall, his gaze holding them in their circulations, his words battering them like a great wind, pushing them and pulling them, threatening to tear them apart entirely, threatening to destroy them entirely, threatening total ecstasy, threatening them with a future of endless circulations, endless spinning, endless energy. Miranda would always slip away from these outbursts of Pentecostal enthusiasm and find some quiet work to do. There was always work to do, although for the women at least, it was not very interesting work.

It was Edna who organized the work for the women. It was Edna who ran things in the kitchen and on the ward. She was in her fifties, short and heavy, strong.

"Sarah, you take Miranda out to garden today and start harvesting those potatoes."

"Shannon, hem the sheets."

"Alice: bedpans."

"Janice and Beverley, those ovens need to be cleaned."

"Alright, girls, bed time."

She would stand beside Albert during their worship services and sometimes he would let her lead them in long, rambling prayers that seemed excessively concerned with righteousness.

"Edna," Sarah whispered to Miranda. "Is the only woman here Albert's never tried to fuck."

It was all very strange to Miranda: all the piety and gendered labour and constant mutual surveillance. Her mom's folks had taken her to church once or twice when she was young, to a dying Episcopalian congregation in the Baltimore suburbs, and she once visited a Baptist Sunday school with a school friend, but her parents were matter-of-factly atheist, not evangelical about it but both capable of withering critique. She grew up thinking of religion as a deliberately indulged in delusion, less harmful than climate change denial but worse than patriotism. Her mom in particular could be acidic about it, about what sort of people claimed moral authority on the basis of revelation, and what sort of people were willing to cede it.

Her mother always put a premium on rationality, on making conscious choices. Miranda's teenage years consisted of a long, agonizing argument with her mother. They fought about her choices of friends, her academic choices, her lifestyle choices. She was never allowed to simply drift with the crowd, to drift through school, to unthinkingly participate in adolescence. It was exhausting: storming out, slamming doors, screaming down the stairs.

"Leave me alone! Leave me alone! It's my life!"

"Yes, Miranda. That is the point. It is your life. You choose to live it. You choose: not me, not your friends, not your culture: you."

And later Dad would come talk to her. Tell her how much Mom loved her, how she only wanted what was best for her, how she naturally wanted her to seize life and live it. It was strange to Miranda to think of her Mom as preaching a sort of carpe diem. Mom who spent all those long nights studying for exams, writing papers, too exhausted to join her and Dad on the camping and fishing trips, to come out to the cottage on weekends, to go catch a Sunday matinee at the mall, and who only got busier after she got the degree and started practicing law. For the longest time she was sure she hated her mother, but she could no longer remember why.

Miranda woke up one night shortly after she got to Big

Echo, uncertain where she was. It took her a few minutes to figure everything out, to make sense of the high ceilings and the ordered cots. She was aware of the women sleeping around her as ill-formed, dark shapes, vegetative, dreaming, and she remembered getting out of bed early one weekday morning in adolescence, sleepy and bewildered, and creeping into the hall to see her mom in the bathroom, getting ready for work. It was early days at the law firm, and difficult for her, lots of fighting with Dad over domestic duties, lots of fighting with Miranda about her needing to pick up the slack around the house. She watched Mom trying on the Ann Taylor pantsuit she bought in the city the last time they visited, chin jutting out slightly with defiance, lips thin and pale with stress. Miranda was fourteen or so, and for the first time in her life she wanted to hold her mom like her mom always held her, to hug her, to caress her hair, to tell her how proud she was of her, how much she loved her. Instead, she slipped back to bed and pulled the clean sheets up over her shoulder, listened to the water running with her eyes closed, listened to the soft, anonymous noise of her mother's ablutions, the hair spray, the squirt of perfume, she lay there and loved her and fell back asleep.

Although they were not supposed to be in the kitchen, Edna endured Ralph and Mitch's regular presence there. They listened to the women talk. And Ralph couldn't keep his eyes off Miranda. The boys mostly soaked up the chatter and the laughter but sometimes Mitch would ask a question or two about the old days, either Little Echo or the very long ago, those days from the deep past, the dreamland of before.

"But there must have been signs?" he asked. "There must have been warnings. God always gives a warning."

"Just the usual," said Miranda. "Crazy guys at the bus station, late night radio preachers, angry uncles."

"You all must have missed it," Mitch insisted. "There's always something."

"Like what?" asked Miranda, "A planetary conjunction? A

choir of angels? Flying saucers?"

"I don't know," said Mitch. "I wasn't there."

"You're right," interrupted Edna. "You don't know and you weren't there. We woke up one morning and everybody was going somewhere, long lines of them leaving the cities and the towns and we didn't know the why or the where of it."

"Didn't you ask them? Didn't you ask them where they were going?"

"Of course," said Edna. "I asked my kids, the first two that left right away, and then the next three after that: "Why? Why? Where? Where?" They just turned around and walked away."

"But what did they say? They must have said something."

"They said nothing. The devil had them," said Edna. "That's all we need to know. We don't need to know why we were saved, why they weren't, we just need to praise the Lord and strive to be righteous."

"That's bullshit, Edna," said Miranda. "We were saved because we're damaged goods. And for that matter, we don't even know if it's us that's saved and them that's damned, or the other way around."

"Doc Smitty and Albert used to talk like you," said Edna. "Down in Little Echo, in the darkness, but once we came up top and saw the light, we saw it didn't matter why, it didn't matter how, it just mattered that we were still here, and the others weren't, and how we're going to live, how we can stay true to the will of God, how we can stay on the path of righteousness."

"But they aren't gone. They're still here, same as us."

"Their bodies are," said Edna. "But their spirits aren't."

Miranda rolled her eyes but kept her mouth shut.

"Where were you before?"

Miranda's cot was next to Sarah's and when they couldn't sleep, they talked.

"I was in Salt Lake City," said Sarah. "My daughter Emma had diabetes and I stayed there until the insulin all went stale. Then after Emma died, I met this guy from Arizona, a sort of a hippy, who was convinced Canada hadn't been hit and was driving north, so I went with him. We got as far as Pocatello and then he died too. I don't know from what. He just didn't wake up one morning. It was too lonely there so I walked to Boise."

"That's a long hike."

"Yeah, it took a couple of weeks or so, and a couple of times I felt like I was going to starve to death, but when I wasn't hungry it was kind of nice, walking down the middle of the quiet highway, thinking about all the people who used to come and go down those roads, all the way back to the pioneers, and before, and how the hills were all still there, unmoved and tranquil, and the wind blowing in my hair. I thought about what happened to everyone, and about Emma. It felt like it was the first time in my life I'd ever had time to think, or even anything to think about."

"Is that when you found God?"

"Don't tease," said Sarah.

"I'm not."

"Really?"

"Really."

"Well," she said. "That's when he found me."

One night, Miranda woke to see Sarah sneaking back into her cot, loose hair falling into her eyes, chemise askew, cheeks flushed from the night air. The next morning as they peeled potatoes she asked Sarah if she'd been up to see Albert.

"Yup," she said.

"Why? Has the old goat got you convinced it's your duty?"

"I like a good fuck now and again. What's wrong with that?"

"Nothing," said Miranda. "Sorry, it's not my business."

"That's right, it's not."

In the afternoon Sarah got in a fight with one of the other women. They screamed at each other until Edna called them a couple of dirty sluts and that shut them up. For a few days Sarah didn't speak to anyone except her little boy.

3

MIRANDA STARTED WORKING OUT ON the range with the boys. She didn't ask anyone for permission. She simply left with them one morning, after serving them an early breakfast of oatmeal. Sometimes they'd spend the night around the campfire and she'd tell them stories about the world beyond the foothills.

"I never got a good sense of what the diggings were like on the Eastern Seaboard," said Miranda. "I only saw bits and pieces, scattered fragments. I thought they were pretty large at the time, but they were nothing compared to what was happening in the west and farther down south. Still. Pretty big. Dave knew this epileptic helicopter pilot who flew up and down the coast between Boston and Miami. South of D.C. all the trees were gone, all cleared out right up into the Appalachians, and the ground carved up. Dave went up with that pilot a couple of times and he said from the air it looked like a crazy, intricate weave of grooves, like if you kick open a rotted old log the termites have been at."

"Was anybody still living there?"

"Well, Dave thought so, thousands of people starved, but he figured the rest were a sort of frontier, slowly sweeping up over the mountains to hook up with the Midwestern works. But that wasn't the part of the story that interested him."

"What did interest him?"

"The epileptic helicopter pilot. He was obsessed with turning him into a joke but he couldn't decide if he was better as the setup or the punchline."

"Were you in a relationship with Dave?" Ralph asked.

Miranda laughed.

"I don't know," she said. "Is living with some guy in a van for a couple of months a relationship?"

One morning, Mitch and Ralph took her down the trail to the graveyard. About thirty wooden crosses were organized into three rows on the eastern face of a hill. You could see for miles.

They watched the clouds cycling south, the wind trailing after them, whipping up dust.

"Dad likes to bury them right before the dawn," said Mitch. "We sing hymns as the sun rises."

"Your dad likes a bit of symbolism, doesn't he?"

"I suppose."

The trail continued north past the graveyard and then sank out of view.

"Where's the trail go?" asked Miranda.

"The old mine," said Mitchell. "An old underground mine. We call it Little Echo but that's not its real name. We lived there when we first got here, when I was small. Dad and Doc Smitty and some of the others thought if we were deep down underground the radiation or whatever wouldn't reach us and the kids would stay normal."

"Didn't work?"

"No, my cousin Jerry was visited when he was fourteen. They tried to keep him down there, to cure him."

"What happened?"

"I dunno. I can't remember it very well, any of it, nobody talks about it much. It was before we got religion, when we still believed in science and shit. Or at least Dad and Doc Smitty did."

"How far is Little Echo?" asked Miranda.

"Two hour walk," said Mitch. "But Dad doesn't like us to go."

It was hot and stagnant. No breeze blew down from the mountains to cool the earth and the air lay on the world like a sleeping thing. Tempers mercurial, arguments constant, Sarah depressed. In the evening she would collapse into her bunk exhausted, and if Miranda was there, she would talk endlessly about the world that had passed away. If Miranda was out late Sarah would fall into a restless sleep, Jesse's slick body next to her, the fringe of his hair damp with their sweat, sheets coiled like snakes at their feet, a hint of the pieta about them.

Edna was fighting with one of the women, one who was pushing back, a favorite of Albert's. Shannon, who came all the way up from Florida looking for Christian companionship, and when she found it, marinated in a state of perpetual disappointment: she complained to Edna about the other women not carrying their weight, and to Albert about Edna overstepping her authority, and to the other women about Albert's unwillingness to more closely manage the politics of the kitchen and the ward.

"I don't know how you managed to get out of the kitchen," she said to Miranda.

Miranda shrugged.

"Every other woman in this place has to slave over the stove tops," Shannon said. "Everyone else has to empty bedpans."

"Do they?" asked Miranda. "Why is that?"

The next day Albert hunted Miranda down. She was shoveling all the shit out of the chicken coop. He was flushed and angry. His voice was raised from the beginning of their discussion and it kept getting louder and louder. Eventually Ralph and Mitch appeared from the machine shed to watch.

"I'm not working in the kitchen anymore," said Miranda. "There's already too many hands in there and Edna hates me. Besides, the boys need help with the outside work."

"It's not your choice," said Albert.

"Whose is it?"

"The community's."

"The community's?" Miranda laughed. "You and Shannon are the only ones upset about it. Even Edna doesn't care. Just you and Shannon. The other women don't care, not enough to say it to my face. Nor do the boys."

"We have things arranged as we do for a reason, Miranda, we need order and discipline to survive."

"I'm shoveling shit and baling hay because I don't care for doing dishes with your squabbling women, Albert. It hardly constitutes a revolution."

"You are diminishing my authority!" Albert shouted.

Later, Mitch said: "Me and Dad sometimes take them sheep and potatoes and corn. To trade for gas."

Mitch, Ralph and Miranda were out near the buffalo jump looking for cattle and stopped to have lunch.

"None of them ever talk, they just stare, and Dad unloads the food and takes the fuel and then we go. I know they take the food because sometimes I go back and watch. I sneak up to the camps. Watch them. They never talk. Never."

"It's so creepy," said Ralph.

"I don't mind them," said Mitch. "They seem so calm, and they're always looking sleek and well-fed, this lot anyways, some of the earlier groups looked a little thin and threadbare, but these ones now, they're like hutch rabbits. They're the hutch rabbits and we're the wild ones."

"They got their system going pretty good," said Miranda. "It was a little hit-and-miss in the first years, I think. There was famine and disease. But right now those trucks roll up and down the old interstates, night and day, all year long, bringing fuel from the Gulf and the Great Lakes to the diggers, and food from who knows where," said Miranda.

"Pete said back in the day he and some other fellows used to run those trucks off the road. Drag the drivers out and shoot them down," said Mitch. "Before he found God, before he found us."

They ate in silence for a bit, and then Miranda said, "Me and Dave used to rob them sometimes."

"You'd rob them?" Mitch stared at her wide-eyed.

"Sure," said Miranda. "But Dave refused to call it robbery or theft, he said none of that stuff was theirs to begin with, it belonged to all of humanity, not just them. Most days he called it appropriation. Sometimes he called it taxation. Roll a semitrailer across the road, go through their shit when they stopped, take what we needed, let them go when we were done."

"Didn't they put up a fight?" asked Mitch.

"Nope, they sat there quietly in their cabs until we indicated we were finished and off they'd go."

"They never fought back?" asked Mitch.

"They never do," said Miranda.

"Then why would Pete and them go shoot them?" asked Ralph. "Why would he do something like that?"

Miranda and the boys needed to put up some fencing but Albert insisted on a prayer meeting first. She was perched on one of the four-by-fours listening to them sing when the headache came. It felt like a vice was tightening on her skull below her ears. By the time the service ended it was just an ache. When they got back two days later she went to Doc Smitty and he gave her some aspirin and said he'd pray for her.

"Jesus Christ, Doc," said Miranda. "I'd rather you didn't."

"There is no future without prayer," said Doc Smitty.

"The sun'll keep coming up without us. Go down too."

"That's not the future," Doc Smitty smiled. "The future is anticipation, it's hope, it's purpose. These kids are all going off to dig up the earth soon enough, and the regulars are dying out, in a few years there'll be no one left, and nothing here but rusting machinery and empty sheds, and the graveyard. Our only hope is prayer and a merciful dispensation from a greater authority. Only prayer can save us. Only prayer will save us."

"You guys manage to make even optimism depressing."

"Without God it's over, Miranda, it's all over," his blue eyes were watering.

"What's over?"

"Humanity."

"That's only a word, Doc, you're getting yourself all worked up over a word."

When Miranda mentioned the headaches and the aspirin to Sarah, Sarah said: "You know Doc Smitty's not a real doctor?"

"What do you mean?"

"He's just a chiropractor from Boise."

"Shit," said Miranda. "That's worse than useless."

Miranda had been telling the boys Dave's stories: the Dog-

Killing Goat Boy, the Sea Crackers, tales of all the various Post-Apocalyptic Tribes that populated the wastelands of his imagination. Eventually she ran out of material but the boys kept asking her for more, every day while they worked, at every meal. She started telling them Grimm's Fairy Tales, and Hans Christian Anderson stories, campfire stories from her childhood, fragments of scattered myths, bits and pieces from old movies and older books. She would always frame them as things Dave told her because for some reason they liked that, and she did too.

"There's this one set of stories," she heard herself saying to them one day, "Dave called the Host of Happiness House. Every version begins with a traveler escaping from some war-torn place, from a catastrophe, and discovering a quiet, wooded place, in a lost valley, near a river maybe, or a lake, or maybe even on the coast, but this quiet is not a natural quiet. It's eerie, devoid of animals and birds, the insects are gone, and in that place the traveller finds a building, an orphanage, or a hospital, or a mental asylum. Sometimes the place is run down, bordering on the derelict. Sometimes it's pristine, beautiful, shining. In one story it's an old, luxurious hotel overlooking a windswept Atlantic beach. But in all the stories it's occupied by orphans, or cripples, or the helpless elderly or the hopelessly mad."

"Like Big Echo," said Ralph.

"Sure," said Miranda. "Like Big Echo. But there's one critical difference. It's always managed by a single, overworked, but very kindly caretaker. This caretaker takes the traveler in without hesitation. The traveler is fed a good meal, and provided a hot bath and clean sheets, and pleasant conversation, and discovers they are happy, content, at peace with themselves, for the first time in years, and they fall into a dreamless sleep."

"So not actually like Big Echo at all then," said Mitch and Ralph laughed.

"The traveler decides to stay a day or two to help out," Miranda continued. "Maybe a week, maybe longer, maybe even a month or more. And then, one morning the traveler wakes up to the sound of crying, and the children or the sick or the elderly or whoever it is are hungry for their breakfast, or they're con- fused or frightened because the caretaker has not shown up. So the traveller takes care of the morning chores and then goes to look for the caretaker, and finds them hanging from a rafter, or wrists slit in the tub, or brains blown out, or simply gone, vanished."

Miranda stopped talking and the boys got nervous.

"What next?" Ralph finally asked. "What happens next? Is that the end of the story?"

"In some versions the traveler stays," said Miranda, "and becomes the caretaker, and keeps working week after week, month after month, year after year until another traveler finally shows up and the story repeats itself."

"What about the other versions?" Ralph asked. "What hap- pens in them?"

"Miranda?" he said when she remained silent. "Miranda? What about the other versions? What happens in them?"

"Sometimes the traveler just leaves."

She tried to stop telling them stories after that but they kept at her. They kept pestering her about violence and slave women, so she told them what she could. All Dave's gratuitous half-fan- tasies about bands of violent men with harems, and while it was hard for her not to make pointed comparisons to the situation at Big Echo, something held her back, something about Ralph especially. She worried about him, about his anxieties, about his hurt feelings, and she wasn't used to worrying about people in that sort of a way. Not Mitch, though. She didn't worry much about Mitch. Mitch was full of rage; he acted like he'd been robbed of something, and he refused to believe Miranda when she told him his childhood was as enjoyable as the vast majority of the millions and millions of childhoods that preceded it, that it had, if anything, in this wide-open country and brought up with love, been better than most.

"Yeah, right," said Mitch. "OK. Maybe. Maybe my childhood did not particularly lack love. Maybe. I don't buy it. But let's pretend all that love made it OK. Even so, you have to admit this is a pretty shitty puberty, and my adulthood might be even worse."

At night when she was falling asleep, she had a half dream, or maybe a vision, maybe some type of a manufactured memory of Smacksburg and Dave walking away from the fire, down towards the lake, towards the caravan, and Fubar staring at her with a face like damnation. She couldn't shake the feeling she was falling backwards into darkness, and after that she refused to tell any more stories for a week or so, not matter how much they begged. She told no more stories until after Mitch walked away.

Ralph came home crying and said they'd been hunting out near Crooked Creek when Mitch straightened up from the spoor and strode off through the brush to the east. Ralph chased him for a few miles, knocked him down a couple of times, and even pointed the gun at him, but Mitch ignored him, simply kept walking, never saying a word.

"I can't believe he left me here all alone," Ralph said. "I can't believe he left me."

Albert grabbed a shotgun, hopped on a four-wheeler and took off. He was back the next day looking exhausted, stretched thin. He went straight up to the admin building and didn't come out for three days. When he did emerge he looked older, bent, head thrust forward, a bit of a shuffle in his walk. It took him a week or two to get his energy back, to start ordering people about again, to start barking at Ralph, to start holding forth about Abraham and Isaac and the sacrifices God demands.

"Mitch couldn't wait," Ralph told Miranda. "He prayed every night that the next day the Devil would take him. He couldn't wait."

"What about you?"

They were sitting next to the tractor eating potato salad and cold sausages.

"I'm so scared," said Ralph. "I don't want to get possessed. I don't want to go to Hell. I pray all the time I'll be saved, that I'll get a tumor or epilepsy or anything, I pray for it all the time."

He looked at her: "But you don't think that works, do you? Prayer?"

"I've never known it to," said Miranda.

They were still fencing, and it was just as well, because Ralph was sick of everyone at Big Echo, and Miranda was pretty tired of them herself. He kept asking for stories, and Miranda was so worried about how depressed he was, she started telling them again. But this time, she tried to come up with more cheerful anecdotes than she had in the past. She made up stories for Ralph about some kids on a barge in the Great Lakes, making their way to the headwaters of the Mississippi, making their way down south, to warm weather, to orange groves and beaches and scuttling crabs, and he was intrigued. He kept asking about the girls, what they looked like, how tall were they, were they Christian, did they have boobs or were they too young. She told stories about them sailing up the Detroit River and through the wild, empty sprawl of the ancient city, the old towers shimmering in the sun. She talked about how they broke into a public library and filled the barge with books. She said they rescued some cats and a dog and had chickens running about on the deck, grew tomatoes and basil and zucchini in boxes and potatoes in rain barrels. She described their long, meandering tour up the east coast of Michigan, the sun on the water and the kids cannonballing off the barge. She told him about the sound of the wind in the aspen trees when they camped, about freshwater fish with their clear eyes, about white meat flaking off translucent bones, about blueberries, fat, warm, and sweet, about how they would read stories to each other at night and how they would fall asleep to the sound of quiet voices and the water against the side of the barge. She told him about Mackinac Island, how the kids knew all the myths about it, the stories and the legends and the histories, how it was sacred to the Anishinaabe people, that it was the first land to appear after the Great Flood. She told Ralph about how the kids would tell each other stories about missionaries and fur traders and soldiers. About rich folk from Detroit. And she started to tell him about how it was when she went there as a child, her, Miranda, to Mackinac with her Mom and Dad, the long humming transit across the bridge to the upper peninsula, the ferry ride, the busy streets with their horses and carriages and the bustling little harbor, but as she stopped talking about her imaginary kids and started talking about her own life, her own experience, her own memories, the words dried up and she was overwhelmed with a vivid vision of the streets as they must be now, and she stopped short. She could clearly see how empty the place was, the streets empty of everything but the wind, the lifeless houses and restaurants and the grand white hotel like a ribbed whale stranded on a graveled beach, and the stables piled high with the bones of the horses that starved to death in their stalls.

"You were there? What was it like?" Ralph asked. "What do you remember?"

"It was lovely," Miranda said. "There was ice cream. I remember strawberry ice cream."

And so they talked about that, about strawberry ice cream in particular and all the other ice cream in general. She started to talk again about the kids on the barge, how they would have sailed under the big bridge and found the initials of all those long-dead lovesick teenagers spray-painted onto the concrete supporting walls, how they would have gone sailing down Lake Michigan as the leaves began to turn, how they would have navigated the canal locks, how, even as Miranda was telling Ralph about their quiet adventures, they must have reached the headwaters of the Mississippi and begun the final leg of their glorious journey to the golden south with its peaches and its pecans and its endless summer sunshine.

A few days later Miranda hiked out past the graveyard and down what was little more than a deer trail through a scrubby, leafless wood. The old compound was overgrown: a tangle of twisted poplars, chain-link fence, and corrugated steel. The head of the mineshaft was a mound of rusted iron, cinderblock, and rubble. She poked around for a while and when she looked up Pete was watching her. He looked even leaner than usual, his matted hair hung in his eyes and down his back, and he was leaning on a crooked walking stick.

"Hey, Pete," said Miranda and he walked over.

"We dynamited it when we left," said Pete. "We made it a tomb."

"Who for?"

"A mausoleum."

"For who, Pete? Who's down there?"

"They're dead: just skulls and bones. They carved their messages into the hard walls with their soft fingers, flesh on stone, we tried to save them, me and Doc Smitty, we drilled holes in their heads to let out the radiation, but it was too late."

"You and Doc Smitty?"

"We buried them all; they'll never get out; they'll never signify. Kill us first, they told us, they begged us to kill them before it got them, don't let us turn, don't let us walk, don't let us dig. We tried to read their minds, we tried to understand, unpack them, pick them apart, but we could not. We tried but we could not."

Miranda could hear shouting and hollering from the machine shed. She walked in and saw a crowd at the other end. Ralph was kneeling before the congregation, arms akimbo, Edna holding tightly onto one, Sarah the other. His face was perfectly impassive, he was staring straight ahead, unfocused, patient. Albert was standing behind him with one hand on the boy's head, the other gripping a leather bound bible.

"Lord Jesus, purify this child," Albert roared. "Keep him safe from evil, keep him safe from the Devil's designs."

"Jesus save him!" someone shouted.

"Lord Jesus, hear our prayer and bless this child!" Albert roared. "Keep him whole! This child who we love. We implore you! We beseech you! Keep his soul at home! Do not let the

Devil steal him!"

"Dear God!" they shouted. "Blessed Savior!"

They were all soaked in sweat, hair wet, clothes plastered to their bodies. They clapped and danced, they raised their hands to the corrugated curved arch of the shed. They begged God to have mercy on Ralph, they begged him to send a cleansing wind to wash the boy clean, they begged him, but God sent them no sign that he heard.

Ralph waited, staring straight ahead at nothing in particular, calm, all the anxiety gone, all the shame and fear gone, perfectly relaxed, perfectly at peace, resigned to waiting until he could go, ready to walk away as soon as they would let him, willing to wait days, months, years. Because he would walk, out to the diggings, there was nothing they could do to stop him except kill him, or lock him up until he died, and every one of them in that building knew it, everyone knew they had already lost.

Doc Smitty was at the edge of the congregation, close to the door, shaking and trembling. He saw Miranda. They stared at each other for a second, then she turned away. As she walked through the compound, towards the gate, she heard them start to sing.

4

NO GUN, NO FOOD, NO WATER, AND LOST. On the second day the buzzing flies led her to a dead fox; the taut hide warping over hips and shoulders, nothing left of the eyes but ragged dimples. She was hungry enough that she considered eating it, but when she pushed it over with her foot she was confronted by an undulating mass.

They had cleaned the ribs bare and were burrowing into the cavity.

"Alive with maggots," she heard Dave say. "Crawling; swarming; stricken; blown with ostentatious maggots."

He followed her as she walked away.

"I keep having dreams about Smacksburg," she told him. "He keeps telling me you're no better than he is. That you two are the same thing."

Dave said nothing.

"Maybe they aren't dreams," said Miranda and she felt like the heavy hot air was pressing her down. She felt like if she gave up and lay down it would flatten her out, push her down into the dirt, melt into her contours, all the pressure crushing her against the ground. She thought of the contorted shapes of flying dinosaurs trapped between layers of sedimentary rock. She thought of dragonfly fossils, mosquitoes in amber.

"Maybe they aren't dreams," she said. "Visions, hallucinations, visitations. It's a good word, isn't it? Visitations. It's Albert's word."

But Dave was not there. Waves of shimmering air rose from the baking hills.

"Affliction," said Miranda. "Tribulation. Retribution."

As she left the hills the land opened up into a grand sweep of prairie, and one morning she saw buffalo, a herd of them off in the distance, a black mass moving over the hills, thousands of them, hundreds of thousands of buffalo, they were moving. She squinted and she could see they were running, galloping, stampeding, they were rushing towards her, over one rise then vanishing behind the next, over that one, and then the next, ever closer, ever nearer, she could hear the rumbling, the thunder of them, of their storm, the storm that was about to break on her, on the land around her. She started to run too, to get away, to escape, but there was nowhere to go, nowhere to hide, so she stopped and turned to face them, but they were no longer there, they vanished, the thunder was gone, the rumbling roar, and nothing came over the last rise but a breeze, not quite cool, but still, a playful movement of the air, pushing the grass about, tickling her sweaty skin, blowing a few strands of hair across her face.

Miranda was camped by a slough, tired and despondent. She

caught a couple of frogs and grilled their skin and bones on an open fire, then dozed off. When she woke she was hungry again and Smacksburg was squatting beside her, watching her out of the corner of his eye. He looked more ragged than before, and his hands and forearms were covered with geometric blue tattoos, a hatchet with a steel head in his belt and an automatic rifle on his back. The necklace around his neck was made of human ears. He looked away and said something but it was indecipherable, like sounds heard while you swim underwater in a pool, laughter from up top, warbling shrieks, the fluid bass of an engine somewhere. He looked at her and spoke again, the words were warped, stretched, the sounds slipped by her. He looked away and pointed to the horizon. She followed his gaze. A thin line of smoke rose from beyond a bluff, no more than a mile or two away.

She squatted in the shadows behind a bulldozer and watched. A half-dozen men and women sat around a fire sharing a bubbling stew. A child played at their feet. Nobody said a word. She hadn't eaten anything in three days besides those frogs, and the smell of the stew, rich with protein and fat, mingled with the tang of gas, oil, and vulcanized rubber, made her shrunken stomach twist. She stood up and stepped out into the circle of firelight. Everyone turned to look at her.

"Please," she said and rubbed her belly. "Please."

The child went back to its play.

"Please," she said but none of the adults moved. She took a step towards them, and another. One of them held out a spoon and she shuffled forward and grabbed it.

"Thank you," she said and looked into the woman's eyes. "Thank you."

She squatted by the fire, shoveled in a few mouthfuls of steaming beans, and felt the burning lump of them sinking into her. She swallowed another few spoonfuls before she thought to roll back on her heels and wipe her mouth and chin clean.

"Thank you," she said but no one paid her any attention.

She followed them as they dug their long looping trenches, their arabesques. No one ever spoke, not to each other, not to the child, and not to her. She worked beside them: cooked the meals, looked out for the kid, set up and broke down the camps, drove the fuel truck after the heavy machinery, down into the labyrinthine canyons they carved out of the earth. Sometimes the headaches would be too much for her and they'd move on without her, leaving her in the sleeping bag they gave her, by the ruins of their fire. She would lie under the big sky and wait to die but the agony would pass. She would eat whatever breakfast they left her, roll up her sleeping bag, and trudge after the crew. They never recognized her arrival or seemed aware of her absence. They were followed across the sprawling landscape by a dozen seagulls and a few scrawny coyotes.

She began to experience flashbacks of frightening intensity, hallucinations really, but always rooted in memory. There was an impossible parade of people marching across the prairie as she worked: people performing long completed tasks, acting out barely remembered dramas: Esther skinning the deer, Mary at her puzzles, Eli at his garden, Fubar watching from his shadows. One evening, while Miranda was collecting firewood in a poplar stand, Sarah walked past, carrying freshly laundered linens, and Edna was in the kitchen singing an indecipherable hymn. She would have these episodes once or twice a day. Nothing from before though, nothing from the deep reaches, always from the shallows. Only these recent folks, only the regulars, coming and going, no real order to it, no pattern, and lots of Dave. Dave kept showing up. Walking by. Lying down in the shade. Lots of Dave. Sometimes generic: Dave asleep beside her as she drove. Sometimes particular: Dave standing by the van in the parking lot at Little Big Horn talking to her; she couldn't hear what he was saying but she could remember, he had been chattering away about Custer, comparing him to his epileptic helicopter pilot, quoting Tennyson: "Theirs not to make reply; Theirs not to reason why." Sometimes she wasn't sure if an episode was a memory at all, even if it always seemed like it must be, twice she was transported east of the Mississippi to stand on the edge of a drainage ditch and stare down at white bones, picked clean by the bugs and the birds and the rats. The ditch was filled with bones, in both directions, bones. The weeds were starting to peek out through the rib cages and the orbits. It looked to her as if a thousand people had lain down in the ditch to die. Dave was sitting in the van, a few feet away from her, rolling another doobie, unconscious to this new horror. Then she would remember he was already dead, and find herself back in the empty prairie.

The child was sick, a boy of about four or five. He had been unwell since Miranda joined the work group, cuddled up to his mother by the fire in the evening, huddled up in various truck and bulldozer cabs during the day. Miranda started taking him whenever she could and the mother didn't seem to mind. She would talk to him as she prepared meals, telling him what she was doing:

"I'm making a fire now."

"I'm boiling water."

"I'm soaking the beans."

She jury-rigged a booster seat out of old tires and leather for him and she'd strap him into the passenger seat when she was in the truck. He'd look out the window and point at things and she'd tell him their names:

"Dozer."

"Hawk."

"Grouse."

"Cloud."

"Moon."

"Deer."

"Truck."

"Sky."

"Earth."

He occasionally repeated a word right after she said it, but he learned very little, certainly not enough to use his words independently. "Truck," he knew, and "beans" and "hot." That was about it. It was all Miranda could tell herself with confidence: he had learned "truck," beans," and "hot." He was too sluggish, too despondent, to manage much more. One day she had a headache so intense and so sudden she passed out and drove the truck off the rough road and into a gully. When she came to, he was sitting quietly, head against the glass, looking up at the thunderheads brewing on the horizon.

She often saw Smacksburg. It was different from her other visions when she saw Smacksburg. It was not memory speaking its old language then, it was not the past, she was certain of that. It was something new and not previously imagined, it was from a different place than any of the places she had been, the visions of Smacksburg, from a different time, not the past but not the future either. It was from somewhere Miranda could not quite imagine.

He was usually on his dirt bike, shadowing their journey, but sometimes he dismounted and came right into camp and tried to talk to her. She couldn't understand the strange noises that came out of his mouth. Nobody else could see him. Not even the child. She worried that one day soon the other visions would stop and it would only be Smacksburg: no more Dave; no more Edna, no Sarah, Albert, Mitch, Ralph; no more Adrian, no more Eli, Lois, Mel; no more Esther, no more Arthur, no more Mary. Just Smacksburg.

Everyone else in the camp was asleep. The child was with his mother. Miranda was at the fire and Smacksburg across from her. He was showing her the palms of his hands. They were badly burned. It looked like the fat had melted under the skin and cooled into a chaos of corrugation and pockmarks. When Smacksburg visited her, Miranda could no longer tell if she was awake, or asleep, or in some more liminal state. She would shake her head and rub her eyes. He was trying to talk to her again, his lips twisting, eyes clear, but it was like watching TV through the neighbor's window. Everything felt like it was submerged in a distorting medium, not just the words, not just the noises, but everything, all the objects in the world, all the smells, all sensation. It all seemed to be traveling across miles to get to her, stretched across miles, stretched across light years.

She dreamed Toledo was on fire. It was night and the port and the refinery and the tower were on fire. The tower was a column of blazing light. The barges were drifting down the dark river and they were ablaze as well, floating islands of fire on the black water. The fires were so many and so bright you could not see the stars, the stars were extinguished, they had been put out, the stars were gone.

It was early in the morning and the band moved on without her. Her head hurt, and it was cold, but eventually she had to pee so badly she scrambled out of her sleeping bag. A coyote watched her from up on a rise. When she was done, she blew some life into the previous night's fire. Once it was crackling away, she looked around. They had left her a bottle of water and some cold beans in an old tin can. She stuck the can in the fire and poked through the camp detritus: a bald tire, a torn blue tarp, some empty plastic bottles, and the body of the child. He lay sprawled on his back, stripped of his clothes, eyes wide. She scratched out a hollow in the frozen dirt as best she could. She put the tarp in the scrape and him on the tarp, brushed his eyes shut, arranged him on his side, hands tucked under his head as if he were asleep, and wrapped him up tight. The coyote watched as she gathered all the stones and rocks she could find and piled them over the corpse. There were so few it took her until noon to raise a cairn a couple of feet high. When she was done, she waved her arms at the coyote, shouted absurdities at him – "Go! Go home!" – until he trotted off. She ate the beans, gulped back the water, rolled up her sleeping bag and trudged after the black, tangled trail of clay churned up by the graders and excavators.

It was a beautiful fall day, the sky a glorious blue, the sound of machinery in the distance – trucks shifting gears as they carted the dirt, and the shuffling, grumbling stop-start-stop-start of a bulldozer at work. She heard it all clearly for a change, the waves of sound washing through the shimmering autumn air, she heard them all so busy at their strange labour, and it made her inexpressibly, unaccountably happy.

ROBERT G. PENNER is a Canadian living in western Pennsylvania. He has published short stories in numerous speculative and literary fiction journals under various pseudonyms and is the founder and editor of *Big Echo: Critical Science Fiction* (bigecho.org). He is on twitter @billsquirrell. Robert lives in Indiana, Pennsylvania.